Books by R. Wright Campbell

MALLOY'S
SUBWAY

MALLOY'S SUBWAY

R. Wright Campbell

ATHENEUM   New York   **1981**

Library of Congress Cataloging in Publication Data
Campbell, R. Wright.
   Malloy's subway.
   I. Title.
PS3553.A4867M3   1981   813'.54   81-66021
ISBN 0-689-11181-9   AACR2

For those two rogues,
Brenda and Dennis

MALLOY'S
SUBWAY

1.

They come together like animals, stuffed into cattle cars, sweating inside their hides of wool and leather. They sniffle and snort and cough into one another's faces, but never look into one another's eyes. Look at the ceiling. Look at the swinging handholds popping back and forth on their springs like dangling billy clubs. Look at the advertisements in two languages. Look at the maps of the subway systems. IRT—Broadway—7th Avenue. Lexington. Independent. BMT. Look at the filth on the floors and the graffiti everywhere.

Linus Bean, a young man with disturbingly bright eyes, too much white showing around the black centers, felt the intimate contact of half a dozen bodies.

An old man wearing a duffel coat as dirty as a mechanic's rag, gloves without fingers, and a scarf like a worn stocking coiled around his throat leaned against Linus's hip, transmitting a feeling of squalor right through Linus's cords.

A businessman in a gray broadcloth overcoat with a mouton collar, modified homburg tilted just right on his well-barbered head, kept his eyes glued to the page of the *Wall Street Journal* and wondered how soon it would be before he got his promotion and could give up "goddamn little economies." The car rocked him up against the arm of the roughly dressed young man and, feeling the sudden tension in it, he was pleased to know there was someone else who was fastidious about all the body contact one was forced to suffer riding the subway.

A black man as young as Linus, flat-faced, wide-mouthed, lips as purple as plums, yellow eyes centered with brown dots as dull as slate, breathed like a dying man as he made room for himself with knees and elbows. Short, sharp moves as subtle as the writhings of a snake, meaning to let everyone know he was not to be messed with.

There was a girl, short, dumpy, pie-faced, with eyes like currants, leaning against Linus's other hip. She let him know the shape of her crotch. When he glanced at her she looked back at him as though he had insulted her. He knew better than to look at her again. She might start yelling rape on him.

Part of his back touched another girl. Their bodies kissed and went away, then kissed again. He could feel the weariness in her. Too tired for love. Too tired to care.

The air was sour with too many human breaths. There was no escaping it. He could hear it starting up out of their bellies and lungs, heavy with the moisture of their guts. It came out in gasps and burbles every time the train screeched around a black curve. Every time it braked after roaring into a station.

The Lexington Express thundered into Astor Place. People got on and off, but the ones surrounding him didn't move. They waited dumbly for the doors to close, looking any-

4

where but into someone's face for fear of trouble. For fear they were standing belly to belly and breast to breast with some crazy, some loony, or some bedbug.

He thought about how easy it would be to slip a long thin stiletto, like the ones old Mafia Dons once carried, into someone's flesh. A scalpel like one a surgeon might use deep into the liver. Into the spine between the separate bones.

He remembered old man Meyer, the butcher who owned the shop in a neighborhood where he'd lived when he was a kid. Big German who always wore a straw skimmer. His white apron was always marked with stains left by his bloody fingers. A neat killer. A fastidious dissectionist.

Meyer owned a knife with a pale wood handle, scrubbed and boiled almost white, the blade so often honed on the sharpening rod, worn away against white bones, that it seemed too thin for the job. It winked and twinkled in the light of the fluorescents as Meyer swiped it through muscle and sinew, parting the layers of fat, whispering through gristle.

Little Linus was fascinated by the butchering, the deboning of a roast, the dismemberment of a chicken. He'd stand at the flesh-smelling block, his eyes scarcely above the side of it, and watch bright-eyed as Meyer went about his work oblivious of the attention paid his knife strokes by the neighborhood kid.

Mrs. Meyer noticed. She was heavy-breasted, her white apron generally stainless, demonstrating her gentler services. She sliced the cold cuts on a small singing machine that was still, even in an age of electricity, turned by hand. She served out sweet-smelling pickles from a stone crock, plucking them from their bath with dainty fingers as plump as small sausages. She was given to hugging small children to her bosom and treating them with slices of bologna or salami.

But she made no such overtures toward Linus. She would sometimes watch him as he stood transfixed by her husband's work. But only for a while. Then she would shiver and tell

5

him to be on his way, to take his purchase away with him to the foster home where he lived.

Linus rocked with the sway of the subway car and thought of Mr. Meyer's knife slipping up between the ribs, into a heart.

The train pulled into the 14th Street station. The young black man shoved his way out. The man with the *Wall Street Journal* looked into Linus's eyes and smiled softly as though they were the only two in the car who had any manners. Linus didn't return the smile and the businessman quickly looked at his paper again.

The train whipped by 23rd and 28th Streets. At about 33rd, Linus slipped the knife out of his pocket without anyone the wiser. The train rocked and crashed against the keepers. The bodies crushed into the car came together softly. He pointed the knife and let the train do the work.

He moved smoothly, politely toward the doors, a nice-looking young man roughly dressed in clean cord pants and a woolen mac, a blue and white striped scarf around his shoulders.

When the express pulled into Grand Central he was one of the first of a crowd of riders to get off. The businessman in the gray broadcloth coat with the mouton collar fell down on the filthy floor. His homburg rolled away. A gout of blood erupted from his mouth.

No one screamed, but someone did remark that the man might be dead.

He was the first.

2.

The cops stood around rubbing their woolen-gloved hands together asking the friction to light fires that would warm them all the way down to their feet. It was a cop's feet that suffered. Hot, pinched, and sore in summer from the miles along the sizzling pavements, dead cold in winter from standing in doorways where puffs of steam heat fooled their faces that it was spring.

They were mostly black. One was a Jew everyone called "Honker." He never objected. Everyone knew that he hated the name and was saving up a poke to have the offending nose bobbed. It made his eyes seem close together, almost crossed in their efforts to see around it. They were intelligent and shrewd. He saw the two burly men approaching. There was a third, slightly smaller, man in tow. Honker stepped forward, touching a finger underneath his stripes as though

7

making certain everyone knew he was the uniform in charge.

The two bigger men looked like plainclothes dicks. They couldn't have been anything else. No doubt when they first started toddling they'd walked with their bellies thrust out belligerently, their hands tucked away in their diapers, heads thrown slightly back, already suspicious of everyone and everything.

They were called "The Twins" by their fellow officers, although they didn't look anything alike except for the stride and aggressive manner. One was an Irishman nicknamed "Gertie," the other a West Indian, with a cultured, high-falutin' voice, called "Limey." They were a team.

The third man walked like a cop, not a detective, although he was in plain clothes. His name was Martin Malloy and that's how everybody knew him and addressed him. One or the other, Martin or Malloy. No nicknames. No affectionate or easy familiarity.

He'd been a uniformed officer of the NYPD. Ten years before, when he was thirty or so, some hoodlum had put four slugs in his gut and hip. Took him out of service into early retirement. It was no way for a man like him to live a life. He pulled a string and asked a favor. He got a job with the New York City Transit Authority. The whole system was his beat.

Gertie shouldered his way through the ring of cops and looked down at the dead man.

"What did it?"

"Icepick. Skinny knife, maybe. It hardly don't show in his coat," Honker said.

"Anybody on the platform see the job done?"

"Wasn't done on the platform. Was done in one of the cars of the Uptown Express."

"Then what's he doing laying here?" Gertie rasped. "Who're you?"

"Sergeant Levine."

8

"Why did you drag him out of the train? Don't you know enough not to touch anything at the scene of a crime?"

There was a nasty grin at the corners of Gertie's mouth and a sly look in his eyes, but if he was trying to stampede Honker he was wasting his time. Levine fixed his eyes on a spot in the middle of Gertie's forehead.

"I didn't and I do."

"Who done it then, the goddamn conductor?"

"He says not. He says he wanted to hold the train in the station," Honker said. He made a motion with his head toward the train conductor leaning up against a pillar.

Limey raised his hand as though greeting a friend, and said, "If you please," in his classy voice.

The conductor hauled himself over with an obvious show of annoyance.

"Tell them what you told me," Honker said.

"Again?"

"What's your name, mate?" Limey demanded.

"Charlie Spiers."

"What happened?"

"That guy dropped dead. Somebody came and got me. I was going to tell the driver to shut the train down. People on the train didn't like the idea."

"Why the hell not?" Gertie demanded.

"They wanted to get home."

"Sonofabitch, didn't they care this poor sucker was dead?"

"That's what I said."

"Well, what the hell, then?"

"They said he wasn't tired any more. Didn't care about getting home one way or the other."

Malloy coughed into his hand. It sounded like strangled laughter.

"Something funny, Malloy?" Gertie asked.

"Bob Hope was funny," Malloy said softly, "but he got old."

9

The conductor looked at Malloy, recognizing him as one of the Transit's own.

"I wanted to do the right thing, but some joker asked a couple other guys to lend a hand, and they picked the dude up by the shoulders and the feet and put him out on the platform," Charlie said directly to Malloy. "I picked up his hat and newspaper."

"That all?" Malloy asked.

"Well, there was nothing I could do except tell the train driver to go on and put a call into the cops."

"They put him down right here?" Malloy went on.

"No. I got some help and moved him out of the way best I could. Hell, they would've stepped right on him getting into the trains."

A train stopped in the station right then with a hellish scream of brakes. The doors cracked open and the cars unloaded their contents right on cue as though illustrating Charlie's text. The mass of humanity rushed toward the staircases, whipping through the turnstiles and the barred gates like ball bearings in a pinball machine. Mindless. Sightless. Not more than half a dozen glanced at the dead man lying on his back, his hat on his chest, his hands crossed on his stomach.

"Who laid him out that way?" Gertie asked.

"What do you mean?" Charlie snapped back defensively.

"What do you mean, 'What do you mean?'" Gertie rasped.

"For Christ's sake, Gertie, Charlie here's not on trial," Malloy said. "You the one laid him out decent, Charlie?"

"The least I could do."

"That's right. You find anything?"

Charlie took a step backward and threw up his hands in front of him, fingers splayed, showing his hands empty.

"I didn't touch a thing on him. Just laid him out decent."

"Hey, don't I know that?" Malloy soothed. "His own

10

mother couldn't have done better. I just mean you didn't see a pick or a knife? Any weapon?"

"Cigarette butts, a condom, and a card from a Monopoly game," Charlie said, making a burlesque out of the accuracy of his memory for garbage.

Malloy nodded as though that was no more than expected. He turned away, stopped, looked at Limey and then at the corpse.

"Don't you want to know who he is?"

"Certainly," Limey said, looking haughty.

"Well, maybe you'd better check his wallet before somebody picks his pockets."

"The body won't be left alone, Malloy. We have uniforms here."

"I know," Malloy said. "I know." He took Charlie Spiers by the elbow and walked him off just as another train came roaring into the station.

3.

There were more than three thousand homicides in New York last year. Time was, twenty years ago, when ninety percent of far fewer killings would have been cleared from the books. That's not to say the perpetrators were convicted and sentenced, but they were identified and arrested. Once murders were committed among family and friends. Now a good deal of homicides are what the criminologists call "stranger crimes."

None of these facts did the family of Howard Morrison, the sporadically frugal businessman, much good. His wife went to Manhattan South Precinct twice a day for the first four days after her husband was murdered, demanding in a quiet, hopeless way to know what the police were doing to find and apprehend the killer. There wasn't anyone there who had the heart to tell her the plain fact that the chances of tabbing her husband's murderer were very slim.

She was there waiting to talk to Lieutenant Posner yet another time one day when Malloy walked in. There was something about the woman that made him ask the clerk who she was. When he was told he went over to sit beside her. He told her who he was and that he'd been there after her husband had been slain.

"Are you working on it?" she asked, a certain eagerness leaping up in her eyes.

"I'm just a Transit Authority officer," Malloy explained. "I cooperate when asked, but this sort of thing is outside my jurisdiction and capabilities."

"What 'sort of thing'?" Mrs. Morrison challenged.

Malloy ducked his head, almost as though he were avoiding a blow. It was difficult speaking to civilians. The language they used wasn't the same. Cops and criminals talked one way, and straight citizens another.

"I didn't mean to sound off-hand," he said. "I meant to say I haven't any part of homicide."

"It happened in your subway. Aren't they meant to be safe?"

"As safe as we know how to make them," Malloy said.

"Not safe enough," Mrs. Morrison accused.

"I know," he said, and shrugged. There was no argument or eloquence in him.

"Is anybody doing anything?" Mrs. Morrison hissed in angry sibilance.

"What does Lieutenant Posner say?"

" 'We're doing everything we can,' " she chanted as though reciting from a written page.

"Well . . ."

"But they won't tell me just what it is they're doing to find the murderer of my husband," Mrs. Morrison insisted.

There was a terrible edge to her voice like a line of force holding back a flood.

Malloy glanced toward the clerk, who was busy elsewhere.

"They can't tell you because they don't know what to do. There's nothing they can do. Not a damn thing."

"What do you mean?" she asked, irritation filling her voice, twisting her mouth.

"Your husband was killed by a stranger on a train. Millions of people ride the subways every day. Nobody can be expected to pick one face out of millions."

"There were people all around," Mrs. Morrison insisted. "Surely someone saw the killer."

"Looked at the killer maybe, but didn't see him. If it is a man. You see, it could be just about anybody."

She started to cry then, silently at first, then with abandoned relief. She leaned into Malloy. He put his hands behind her shoulders and patted her back from time to time. After a while she straightened up and took a handkerchief from her purse. She repaired her face as best she could, peering wide-eyed into a little vanity mirror. Then she tried a smile.

Malloy smiled back.

"No help," he said. "But I thought you should know the truth."

"A great deal of help," she said. "I knew the truth, but I had to hear someone in authority say it."

"I'm not in authority," Malloy said.

She patted his hand almost briskly. "Then you should be," she said, and stood up sharply.

"Would things be done differently if Howard had been important?" she commented almost idly.

"It couldn't change anything," Malloy said.

Mrs. Morrison nodded and went out the door.

Malloy sat there and thought about changing things. In the public mind there always lurked the slightest suspicion that cops worked harder when it was one of their own brought down. Legend had it that cop-killers never got away with it.

Well the geek who'd put four in Malloy had gotten away with it. Of course he hadn't actually killed him, but it hadn't been for not trying. That gunman was out there in the streets. Malloy wouldn't know him if he sat right next to him on a train running through the city. The man who'd given him so much pain had been nothing more than a running shadow in the shadows at the end of a long alley.

Sometimes, in dreams, Malloy imagined he could almost make out a face. He only had to get a little closer, but he was afraid to pursue the man into the depths of the dark tunnel.

When he'd been just a kid, eight years old or so, living in the tenements with his mother and his two sisters, one of his chores had been taking the garbage down the seven flights of stairs into the basement. Sometimes it happened that he had to do it after dark. He hated that because the superintendent of the building kept nothing more than a twenty-five watter burning at the top of the cellar stairs. Just enough light to show the way down the steps, but not enough to shine into the dark shadows where the cans were kept.

Even when they were all sitting in the parlor at night and his mother asked him to go out into the kitchen for some reason or other, he would pray that he would find the string that turned on the overhead globe right away. Otherwise, if he missed it on the first pass, he would sweep his hand back and forth in the dark above his head, desperately trying to turn the light on before his racing heart choked him.

He was cravenly afraid of the dark and just as afraid to say so.

One night he decided that he had to do something about it. He went down into the cellar and into the unused coal bin at the very back where the air was so black he couldn't see his hand in front of his face when he held it out at arm's length. He sat down on an old trunk and hugged his knees as the waves of terror washed over him again and again until he thought he would faint.

He didn't. After a long time the fear went away, leaving him weak and shaking, but master of himself.

15

The damned gunman had brought all the terror of the dark flooding back. Nobody knew it, but that was one of the big reasons why Malloy walked the tunnels day and night, proving to himself that he wasn't really afraid of the terrible fear.

4.

The 42nd Street Shuttle looked like an animal farm. Ladies who had once come out strongly against the slaughter of baby seal, beaver, and fox sweated in arctic wolf, mink, and rabbit: the first being vicious, the second ranched, and the last plentiful.

The members of the Hadassah of Temple B'nai B'rith, Mount Kisco, were going home to Westchester after attending the latest Neil Simon play.

A lovely little woman, Mrs. Spector, wife of a Mount Kisco physician, sat down between Mrs. Roth and Linus Bean, who was wearing just a sweater and a scarf.

She smiled her best mother's smile and asked him if he wasn't cold. He shook his head.

"I won't be out in the cold for very long," he said.

Mrs. Spector colored slightly. His voice was like velvet,

deep yet somehow fragile, as though he suffered some Victorian weakness of the chest. She contented herself with the feeling of his youthful leg against hers as she chattered on to Mrs. Roth about the deep insights buried in Simon's one-liners.

Mrs. Roth tossed that out for general discussion. It became a happy babble as the women, sitting and standing, rocked in and out, this way and that.

Linus looked at the scrawl and tangle of graffiti on the walls and windows of the car. He felt himself smothered in fur and strangled by a riot of scents. He shuddered like a dog.

Mrs. Spector felt the tremor and turned to him as the ladies chattered on. She was about to tell him that he should go right home, take a hot bath, fix a steaming lemonade, and get right into bed. Instead she said, "Oh, dear," as she felt a strange little stab in her side. Then she sighed and leaned a bit more heavily on Mrs. Roth. Her head tipped over to one side and lay into the collar of her mink.

Linus got up and made his way casually to the side door. The car rocked and rolled, slamming against the keepers. He didn't see Mrs. Spector keel over into the place where he'd been sitting, but he heard the change in the tone of the voices around her.

At Grand Central he stepped out onto the platform and waited for a minute. Then he stuffed his scarf under his sweater and went back inside the car. Mrs. Roth, Mrs. Gottlieb, and three other ladies were fussing around Mrs. Spector. They kept saying, "This is our stop, dear," and "Aren't you feeling well, Sadie?"

He took the dead woman by the arm.

"Help me," he said.

Mrs. Gottlieb, a woman twice as big as he, put an arm around her friend and together they got her out to a bench on the platform, the toes of her pumps making streaks in the dirt.

18

Linus offered the suggestion that she be placed on her back. He put her big purse under her head to make her more comfortable. He crossed her hands on her stomach. He slipped a Monopoly card into her coat pocket. Then he walked away as her friends crowded around her.

After a little while Mrs. Gottlieb recognized death.

By the time Malloy got to the scene, Mrs. Spector still hadn't been disturbed. The look of her lying there as though already laid out in her coffin gave him a chill. That and the similarity to the man who'd been casually murdered five days before.

It didn't take a genius to know that a killer was loose under the streets of Manhattan.

5.

Bo Wango shuffled along the Con Ed steam tunnel, his cardboard case of bits and pieces under his arm. Once he'd been a merchant with a shop on Mott Street. That was lost now, along with a wife and two kids. Sometimes he had to stop in his tracks when such thoughts came to him so that he could peer at them and sort them out. He knew he'd lost the shop because of no business. Where he'd lost the wife and kids he sometimes couldn't remember. At other times he knew that the son had been killed in war and the daughter lost somewhere in the city. The wife had simply died one day.

After that he'd been a rubber man selling toy balloons in the park, a flawny man with a suitcase full of trashy jewelry, and even a bug man, vending little chameleons one summer when they were all the rage.

He'd been a high pitchman those days, working the

20

streets without license, running when the cops came his way. Life had been pretty good on the curbstones.

Now he sold bits and pieces from time to time, but never on the streets, always in the tunnels, shuffling along, counting the corners from manholes overhead and talking to himself.

He passed Linus in the tunnel.

"Where you been, Linus?" he asked.

"Here and there," Linus replied, and walked on, head down. There was a puzzled expression on his face as though he had just acted against his nature and had been startled by it.

"Here and there," Bo Wango muttered. "Here and there. That's what passes for civil greetings nowadays. Here and there."

The words echoed in Linus's head, a Doppler effect of memory, changing in pitch and intensity, but persisting all the same.

"That's my life," he murmured to himself. "Here and there."

The woman on the train had been trying to be kind to him. Motherly. She'd been concerned about him or, at least, had pretended to be. Why had he knifed her then? It wasn't often in his life anybody had been very kind to him, concerned about him. There had been moments, of course. Very few can claim a life suffered without even a stroke or two. But just caring, just being kind, had never had much effect upon him. It never lasted. After kindness came unconcern. After caring, carelessness.

There'd been one foster home he'd lived in that was on a tree-shaded street in a nice old section of South Brooklyn around Smith and Ninth. The natives call it Red Hook. The public grammar school was just a couple of blocks away, close enough for nine-year-old Linus to walk to it alone.

He was used to being a loner, used to being the stranger, alien and suspect. He'd already been to seven schools before he hit the fourth grade. They'd been a mixed bag, but nothing like the school in Red Hook. The kids weren't wary, but aggressive and violent.

One day, Linus came home with his legs kicked and bruised. The man and woman who were paid by the juvenile authority to take care of him didn't have much to say about it.

The wife made a big thing about putting some of her sweet-smelling bath salts into the water of his tub that night, and clucked her tongue a lot, but though she said she cared that the kids had ganged him, she really didn't know what she could do about it.

The husband felt Linus's spindly arms and legs, hurting the black and blue marks all over again, and said that he'd have to teach Linus how to handle his mitts, then went behind his newspaper and told Linus to run get him a can of beer.

The second and third time Linus came home wounded it was more of the same. The next time, the woman roused herself enough to compose a note, with much difficulty, demanding that the teacher take better care of the children put into her charge.

Linus handed it over to the teacher after class. She looked at it, read it twice, glanced at the boy's battered legs, and pinched the spot on the bridge of her nose between her eyes where the worst of her headaches always started. She tried to explain, as patiently and as kindly as she knew how, that she couldn't be everywhere, couldn't take on the responsibility of policing the playground, or the protection of every child in every corner of the school; she couldn't "goddamn well be a cop." When she started to cry, her face screwed up in something like rage, Linus just walked away.

The bad thing was that one of his tormentors had been lurking in the cloakroom and heard it all. When Linus got out to the concrete-surfaced playground surrounded by chain-link fence, nearly deserted now at the end of the school day, two lines of eight-, nine- and ten-year-old kids were waiting for him. Girls and boys. Some as skinny and frail and afraid as he. They linked their arms at the elbows and started toward him, lashing out with their feet in unison like a miniature chorus line, evil little Rockettes hoofing it up at the Music Hall.

"We're the kicking machine," they piped out. "We're the kicking machine. We're the kicking machine." Their feet hit the pavement as though they wore jackboots. "We're the kicking machine."

"We're the kicking machine!" they chanted, coming closer and closer, hemming Linus into a corner, against the red bricks with nowhere to go.

Then, after an age, the words were changed.

"We're the killing machine! We're the killing machine!" they cried.

The man and the woman paid attention then, after Linus was put in hospital. The teacher and the principal paid attention then.

When Linus got out of the hospital he was sent back to Juvenile Hall to await replacement. He was said to be a boy who attracted trouble and violence.

"Here and there," Linus murmured to himself. "Always here and there." He spun around on his heel.

"Here and there, goddamn it, that's where I've been!" he shouted after Bo Wango.

6.

Bellevue Emergency starts warming up about six o'clock on Friday evening. Nothing really hot. Just the weekend athlete getting an early start after the last day at the office. Two martinis and a fast game of handball. Heart attack sport for the overweight and underexercised.

One or two ethnics who'd fallen under the knife. Early evening brawls over some baby *putas*. Old gang vengeance that couldn't wait for dark.

Drunks sick on smoke. A battered wife. Sometimes a battered husband too drunk to defend himself against the wife he'd beaten up once too often. Some old dear, living out of a shopping bag, picked up in the gutter lying in her own mess, ancient legs covered with sores. Some of them ulcerous and eating down into the bone.

By midnight Emergency is hell, with no relief in sight

from God or man until Monday morning rolls around and the sweeper shoves the vomit-stained paper towels, the pieces of clothing cut away from wounded limbs, the bloody rags and wads of cotton into a pile for burning. Sometimes a lost piece of human flesh gets swept up with the rest.

Irma Sweet was charge nurse on the swing shift. From four until midnight she ran the ward all hard-eyed and efficient in her cotton bra and panties, space-ranger orthopedic shoes, and the butcher's apron that was her special uniform. One she would not put aside despite constant reminders of hospital policy from Public Relations.

"Butchers get bloody," she told them, and went on her way, pushing the blue-blazers aside if they didn't get out of her way.

Doctors new to the service thought her too big for her britches, cotton or otherwise. Old hands knew that Irma, working triage, had an eye for the ones about to die no matter what, and had the guts to shift them off to the side to make way for the ones who could be helped. She knew the repeaters and could spot a malingerer new to the game, sniff out a hophead across the room, and recognize an asshole when she saw one.

Every Friday night she started out thirty-five and closed out Sunday looking seventy.

When Malloy picked up Irma Sweet at twelve o'clock Sunday night she wasn't wearing cotton underdrawers or orthopedic shoes. She didn't look seventy.

She was slick in a silk blouse and tartan skirt, her legs cased in nylon, her feet in open-toed high heels and damn the weather. She wore a scarf Malloy had bought for her their first Christmas. She had a fake fur chubby against the cold.

They went to a movie and had some Italian food in a little family restaurant on Broome Street in the heart of Little Italy.

When they got back to her flat in the East Village he un-

25

dressed her very slowly, cuddling her on his lap when she was down to her garter belt and underwear. It was lacy and clinging and altogether frivolous.

When she wore it for him he always said that she had the sweetest ass, and that pleased her in a way she could not describe.

His hands were big, even for a man who was in no way small. They completely cupped her behind when he stood up, her legs going around his waist and her arms around his neck.

She ran her tongue up the side of his jaw and touched the lobe of his ear.

"Hey, mister," she teased, "why don't you take your coat off and stay awhile?"

He laughed. It was thick laughter, as though he were choking. He set her down on the floor very gently as though she were something very fragile.

She helped him out of his clothes. She dropped them on the floor, anywhere.

He backed her toward the bed until she felt the backs of her knees touch the mattress. She fell back, letting him do the work of setting her down easy.

His mouth was all over her. All at once he was in one hell of a hurry.

"Lover," she sang softly like a dockside whore.

When they were spent, they lay back on the rumpled sheets, sweating heavily.

The steam heat made the air in the room heavy.

"Christ, isn't the super ever going to fix the valve on that radiator?" Malloy asked.

"Ask me in the summer."

"Hot as the Gobi in here," Malloy complained. "Can't we open a window?"

"After we cool down a little. When we're ready to sleep," Irma said. She patted his thigh.

"You're mothering me," he said.

"Better than nursing you."

He grunted.

She knew he was testy.

"Okay, what is it?" she said.

"There's a crazy killing people on the subway."

"Tell me about it," she said. "Tell me about crazies. Let's match crazies."

Her voice got thin and rose a little. Malloy took her into his arms.

"I keep forgetting what you do all night," he said.

"I keep forgetting you run around alone in the guts of the city," she replied.

"Ain't we got fun," Malloy whispered into her ear. After they made love again, they both felt easier.

"A little lady from Mount Kisco was killed on the subway this weekend. Going home with her Hadassah girlfriends. Short ride on the shuttle."

"An eighteen-year-old kid died after a car wreck," Irma said. "He had a hard-on when his heart stopped."

"There's nothing much you can do about the ones that come to you, except try to patch them up the best you know how," Malloy soothed.

"You've got to try and stop the loony," Irma said.

He nodded.

"What are the cops doing?"

"The best they know how."

"Yeah, but what?"

"They put out a watch for anybody acting strange as soon as they got the call. It had to be somebody on the shuttle."

"One of a thousand."

"One of a million more likely. The killer could have taken the seven all the way to Flushing or the Lex north to the Bronx Zoo, Dyer Avenue in Eastchester or Pelham Bay Park. Could go north to Woodlawn Cemetery, too. Or he could go south to Crown Heights or Flatbush. That's if he left from Grand Central.

27

"If he took the Shuttle back to Times Square he could grab the IRT and end up . . . let's see," he ticked off his fingers, "Van Cortlandt Park, Lenox Terminal at a hundred and forty-eighth, White Plains Road, South Ferry, Brooklyn College, or New Lots Avenue.

"We got one hell of a transportation system, you know that, Irma?"

"The cops could never block all the exits even if they knew who they were looking for," Irma said. "Don't you brood about it."

She fingered the hair at his ears.

"You still going to that barber in the Columbus Circle Station?"

"I switched to Harry under City Hall."

"Just as bad. You look like it was cut with sheep shears."

"He's still only three bucks. Barbers on the street get seven."

"If a dentist would pull your tooth for a buck with a pair of pliers would you let him do it?"

"It's not the money."

"I know. You better watch it, Malloy. You'll be living underground twenty-four hours a day if you don't watch yourself. Live in the stations and never see the light of day."

She shuddered suddenly.

"What's the matter?" Malloy asked.

"Just so goddamn tired."

"Maybe we shouldn't go out Sunday nights. Maybe it's too much after the weekend."

She clutched him tighter.

"That ward makes me crazy, Malloy. If I didn't get to see you at the end of the shift I think I'd never get sane again. What the hell's happened to the city?"

"Too many people. Just too many goddamn people."

Sometimes as he watched them pour by, Malloy thought about how stunned they looked, their eyes staring and veiled like those of sleepwalkers. It made him nervous and some-

28

how sad. Yet it made him want to know what went on behind the eyes that were so enchanted.

They reminded him of the way people looked coming out of the movie houses when he was a kid, especially after a matinee, when they came out of the dark into the daylight blinking like small nocturnal animals. He remembered how he'd felt so lost and anxious then, as though something of great importance had happened in the world when he'd been hidden away.

When he'd grown older he'd stopped going to the movies, agreeing to do so only on rare occasions when some woman he was involved with insisted on it.

He preferred the passing scenes underground. Fascinated by them, and uncomfortable with the transitions from the tunnels to the open air, he'd come to spend more and more of his time in the tunnels, making the people in them his real community of neighbors.

Irma thought he cared for the society in the subways, but it was just that there Malloy felt at home.

She sighed deeply in her sleep and Malloy went to sleep as well.

7.

When the dream came it cast no shadow before itself. There was no aura of premonition such as those that precede the horror of certain seizures. It didn't matter if the day had gone well or badly, whether it was raining or dry, hot or cold. It attacked when least expected.

It was always the same, practically a perfect reproduction of that night as he remembered it . . .

Feeling fit, Malloy walked along the city streets in uniform, walking a last patrol before he reached his apartment and his wife. It was a pleasure, not a duty. He was regularly assigned to a cruiser.

But every night, at the end of his shift, he liked to take the subway to Clark Street in Brooklyn Heights and walk the rest of the way home to where he lived on Hicks. On the train and along the streets the people looked at him with respect and he smiled back at them, letting them know that he wasn't wearing the blue to hassle them, but to take care. Unlike other cops who changed into civvies before going home, Malloy liked to wear the uniform.

Would it have come out any differently if he'd been in his regular duds that night? Maybe the burglar at the door of the appliance store wouldn't have spotted him for the law. At least not right away, as he did. Maybe he wouldn't have been spooked so badly that he pulled the gun and started blasting away before taking a chance on running first.

The first shot went wild and went zeeing off the sidewalk. Somewhere behind him Malloy heard the sound of breaking glass, but that was only a split-second after he felt the searing pain above his hip bone. The impact spun him around and knocked him sprawling into the filthy gutter. The second shot hadn't missed.

The thief was running then, haring off through the shadows, trying to look back to see if Malloy was in pursuit or setting himself to shoot back. He slammed into a stack of garbage cans. It slowed him down enough for Malloy to make his feet and go stumbling after him.

"Halt!" Malloy sang out, right according to the book. The next bullet seemed to strike him in the very spot the first had entered. The pain nearly blacked him out. He leaned against a corner of a building and thought about giving it up.

"Halt!" he yelled out again and squeezed off two shots just as the runaway disappeared into a side alley. Then Malloy stumbled on, his right hand holding the gun, his left hand clutching his side where the blood ran warm.

He almost walked into the next bullet. It came singing out of the black mouth of the alley, clipping the air by his ear with a sound of a party popper remembered from his childhood.

He hit the ground and bellied around the corner so that he could peer down the alley. He saw the briefest flash of a face staring his way, illuminated by the light that came

31

through a narrow toilet window, encrusted with dirt, through which a saffron electric glow emerged. Then the thief was gone.

Malloy got back on his feet. Hugging the wall he moved down the alley, trying to see a shadow in the shadows. It seemed to take twenty years to make the twenty yards to the rubble and garbage at the end of it. It was a dead end. He hadn't heard the thief jump the fence. When he saw the deep, narrow cellar entry it was too late. He caught two more in the gut and went down for good.

He let out one great, outraged, frustrated scream, angry with himself for having played it dumb.

Through the years, when the dream came upon him in his sleep, Malloy had learned to stifle the scream. By now he caught it in his throat before it could pass his teeth. The pain of it always woke him up. It was like a hand choking him.

He lay there in his own sweat, the sheets coiled around his leg and strangling his crotch. It took a long, careful time to disentangle himself.

He padded silently across the floor into the bathroom and closed the door carefully behind him, making certain that the latch didn't click out in the silence. He ran a whisper of water and bathed his face. He stood in the dark, clutching the sink, his head lowered, and trembled for a long time. Then he went back to Irma's bedroom and got dressed.

Irma never woke. She'd grown used to his getting up in the night. When she found the bed empty in the morning she knew he'd had the dream and had gone out to prowl the subway tunnels, proving his courage yet another time.

In the morning he'd come back and they'd sit down to breakfast together, making small talk, never mentioning his early morning terror.

8.

There are two or three kids, clean-cut and collegiate, who work the stations more or less regularly. Linus knew the spoof and worked it well. It was the way he made the necessary cash he had to have to get along.

He was very slim, and the school scarf gave him a certain picture-book quality, as though he were more than just a nice schoolboy but the very essence of what a nice schoolboy was all about.

His light gray eyes were guileless. His soft brown hair made a nice careless fluff across his forehead. Women were tempted to brush it back. He had a nice mouth, shaped like an infant's, but harder, more than a touch cruel. He could bring embarrassed color to his cheeks on call.

He approached the well-dressed matronly looking woman carrying the well-filled shopping bag.

"Ma'am?"

She stopped short, shied a bit, ready to run or protest this intrusion in her path. Then she saw who it was. A young man who looked like her own son, just ten years before.

"This is very embarrassing for me, ma'am," Linus stammered.

Her eyes narrowed a trifle. There was enough big city shrewd in her to smell a con. She started to walk around him. Linus reached out, then jerked his hand back, his cheeks turning carmine as if he had only just realized that he'd almost committed an unforgivable offense. He started to stutter his apologies.

"Now just slow down and tell me what it is," she said. Her good heart was completely taken in.

"I've never had occasion to do anything like this before," Linus managed. "I'd try to walk it, but I left my coat in the men's room while I was washing my hands and somebody stole it and it's very cold out and we're at Rockefeller Center and I live way out around Forest Hills."

"Oh, my."

"I haven't even got a token. My change was in the pocket of my coat."

The woman handed over two quarters and a dime.

"You really should be more careful," she smiled and then squeezed his hand sympathetically.

"I know, I know," he said and thanked her and brushed the hair out of his eyes.

She hesitated, wanting to savor the moment, the good deed she'd done; then she hurried on.

Linus pocketed the sixty cents. He waited a few minutes. He walked toward the entrance and spotted a man with a young woman on his arm. Linus knew that such a pair was always a good bet. It gave the man a chance to look like a big shot.

He went into his dog and pony act. The man stood there

34

with his feet planted slightly apart the way a fighter does before throwing a punch. The girl looked into Linus's face and then up into the face of her boyfriend.

If it was the last day of the world she'd take Linus, who was young and fair, to bed with her, but it was the first day of the rest of her life and the guy she was holding on to was more than a lover. He was dinner, a show, good times, vacations, and the rent now and then.

"You want money?" the man said.

Before Linus could answer the girl squeezed the man's arm. "Go ahead, Phil, give the kid a dollar. It's cold. We can't let him walk home."

"Oh, he won't walk home, will you, kid? He'll probably take a cab. That is after he has himself a nice meal in some good restaurant. Maybe a couple drinks. Maybe take in a show."

"What are you talking about, Phil?"

"I don't understand, sir," Linus murmured.

"I caught your act last week over at Queensboro Plaza. I got a memory for faces."

"It wasn't me, sir."

"It was you. You were wearing a blue and white scarf. I got a memory for faces."

"What's he do, Phil?" the girl asked.

"He's a beggar. He's got a pretty face and a nice pitch."

"Oh, I can't believe that," she said.

Linus grinned. "He's right. You have a good memory all right."

The girl frowned. She wanted Linus punished. After all, she'd been ready to screw him if it was a choice between him and Phil and it was the last day of the world. She'd been ready to give him her body. And, Christ, she didn't even know him.

Linus turned away, dropping the schoolboy slouch.

"Hold it," Phil said.

He made the gesture a big one. He pulled out a packet of bills folded into a spring clip. He peeled off a fiver.

"Here you go. Have a ball."

Linus stared at the bill in his hand. He folded it up small and tucked it into his watch pocket.

"Well thank you, sir. Very generous of you. Tonight I might even buy *me* a whore."

He went off to the lockers at Grand Central Station. He bought another day's storage for a handful of quarters. He took out his mackinaw and an Irish hat of crushed tweed.

He went down several staircases. He came to places where his footsteps rang hollow from the walls that were slick with moisture. He reached the lowest sub-basement. It was warmer there. He opened a small green door and bent almost double in order to pass through. A light shone at the end of a passageway. It was yellow and warm, not quite homelike, but it would do.

Overhead the frantic activity of Grand Central Station went on, a murmur as of invading legions, punctuated by the frequent rattle and thunder of arriving and departing trains.

"Hello, Linus," old Mumblety Peg said.

She was stirring a stew in a pan set on a pair of steam pipes. Off in a separate little room defined by empty orange crates tied together with twine she had her washing machine. A pail filled with water, detergent, and small clothes. A rubber hose from a valve in one of the pipes forced steam to bubble up in the pail. Peg was very proud of her domestic arrangements and her widely known reputation for cleanliness.

Linus smiled, but didn't speak. He leaned up against the wall and folded his arms, smiling down on the old woman in an affectionate way.

"What are you making?" he finally asked.

"Supper," she said flatly, and cut her eyes at him.

He waited a long moment and then asked what was in it.

36

"Venison," she lied. "I shot a deer in Central Park."

"What with?" he asked after another long pause.

"With a rubber band and a paper clip. Caught him right between the eyes."

"You know you can get arrested for that?"

"Only if they catch me." Peg laughed.

He squatted on his haunches beside her. They looked like people must have looked crouching in the caves before they got ambitious.

"You want to eat?" she asked.

Linus looked at her as though trying to figure out what it was going to cost him. Finally he came right out with it.

"How much?"

"A game," she said.

"What game?"

"Monopoly."

"That takes so long," he complained. "How about backgammon? A set of three?"

The old woman set her lips in a stubborn line. She looked into the pot as though he weren't there.

He dipped his head and smiled at his feet.

"Okay."

After they ate the Mulligan, Mumblety Peg set out the grimy board, stacked the worn cards in the proper spaces, started to lay out the property cards.

"You're the banker," she said.

"Wasn't I the banker last time?"

"No. You took care of the real estate last time," she said, bristling as though he were already trying to cheat her.

He took the greasy, soiled play money she handed him. Some were merely bits of notepaper, cut to size, with the proper denominations printed on them in crayon.

She continued laying out the cardboard deeds.

"Damn," she said.

"What's the matter?"

"Somebody's stealing pieces of my game."

"Now, who'd want to steal pieces of a ratty, worn-out old Monopoly set?" he asked.

"I don't know, but last week it was Short Line and Park Place missing. Now it's Oriental Avenue." She looked up at him slyly. "Maybe it's you stealing my cards."

"My God, Peg, why would I want to do that?"

"So you wouldn't have to play with me when I give you supper."

"You know I wouldn't do anything that mean," he said with the light sincerity he used so well.

Peg simpered and bridled like a young girl.

"I was only teasing," she said. "It don't matter. I'll just make us another one."

She took a handful of used wax crayons from the pocket of her apron. She drew a blue band on the top of a piece of cardboard and lettered Oriental Avenue under it in black. Down at the bottom she put the price, "$100."

The game lasted two and a half hours. Linus gave it away at the end.

Two days later a black teenager named Philo Lincoln was stabbed to the heart in a 7th Avenue Express train. This time the train was held in Park Place Station.

9.

Gertie sat on a wornout subway car seat with Limey next to him. They were in their hats and overcoats, their hands idle in their laps. Limey held a folded newspaper.

When Malloy stepped into the car he thought they looked like a couple of tired old commuters.

At the other end of the car a group of men were busy around something on the floor. They shifted, grunted, and moved about without standing all the way up. Like a bunch of ducks. A photographer grabbed angles as though he were going for a Pulitzer, composing shots for drama. When the blue strobe went off it sent a pain into the center of Malloy's brain. He hated headaches.

Malloy watched for a while. From time to time he saw a foot. The dead man was wearing a runner's athletic shoe, electric green and yellow. Malloy wondered if the dude had ever jogged through Central Park up around Harlem, or if the shoes were just for flash.

There was some activity outside the end of the car, too. A heavy metallic clang announced that the coupling had been disengaged. The car rocked once. The lighted train in front of them pulled away.

Malloy went to sit opposite the detectives.

"How many crazy people do you think are riding the trains every day?" Gertie asked Malloy.

"How many people use the subways?" Malloy replied.

Gertie grunted. "You're right. We're all a little nuts."

They glanced up the car toward the activity around the dead man. There wasn't much they could say to one another. Nothing sensible. The casual killer, the motiveless homicide, left them with no end of thread to take up in their fingers.

Transit mechanics worked on the coupler at the other end of the car. A donkey engine came up and hooked on. It pulled the single car down toward the black mouth of the tunnel and off to a shunt line. The regular train rocked back along the track to join the other half. After it took off in the right direction, the engine and car that was left jerked as though they were anxious to get going too. The doors to the car started to close.

A tall, thin character with a nose like a knife blade and a jaw like the head of an ax slipped through at the last second like a curl of smoke. He sat down next to Malloy, hands in pocket, as though he were aping the Transit cop or playing like his shadow.

"Hello, Seagrave," Malloy said.

"Hello, Malloy. What have you got for me?"

"It's not mine. Homicide's not mine."

"You just cooperating?"

"A little more than that, maybe. After all, somebody's messing up my living room."

The skinny man was a newspaper reporter working his

40

own featured column, "City Shadows," after twenty years on the crime beat. Rumor had it that he went to bed only two hours a day and one of those was taken up screwing any one of a number of hat check girls, hookers, or Salvation Army soldiers. He had a soothing, off-handed way about him. People spilled their guts to him and never realized they were giving away secrets.

The donkey engine pulled the single car along the track at a pace that seemed funereal. The train seemed light and insubstantial to those who rode in it. A death train.

A sergeant from forensic walked the length of the car, anticipating the rock and roll like a sailor never come ashore. He carried a common shoebox in his hand.

"Whatayagot?" Gertie asked without looking up.

"We'll count the matches and the butts, the rubbers and the peanut shells when we get the car to the barns. We might learn something more from the photographs when we have time to study them. This is a rough collection."

"You chalk their positions on the floor?" Limey asked innocently.

"You putting me on?" the sergeant said.

Limey grinned.

The sergeant said, "You're a comedian," and shoved the box at Limey, who waved it away.

"Give it to the senior officer," he said.

"Who would that be?"

"Detective Walsh here. This gentleman right here."

"He means me," Gertie said.

He poked a finger around in the collection of things that were bigger than a scrap of paper or a cigarette end.

"What the hell's this?" Limey asked.

He held up a property card from a Monopoly game.

"That's a piece of a game called Monopoly," Gertie said. "You got that, it means you bought Oriental Avenue."

"Can I see that?" Seagrave murmured. He bent over and reached across the aisle, sniping the piece of cardboard out of

41

Limey's fingers like a wink.

"Don't do it, fachrissake," Gertie said.

"Do what?" Seagrave responded.

"Don't give us any fucking labels. None of that 'Zebra Killings' or 'Son of Sam' shit."

"It wouldn't be bad, Gertie," Seagrave said, taking out his pad and pencil. " 'The Monopoly Killings.' What's your true first name, Detective Walsh?"

"Golder."

"What?"

"A family name."

Seagrave asked that it be spelled and wrote it down. "Yours, Detective Whittlesey?" he said to Limey.

"Maurice."

"I don't have to ask you yours, Malloy," Seagrave said, looking at the Transit cop. "Hey, hey, hey," he said, meaning to catch Malloy's attention.

Malloy kept staring at the card Seagrave had returned to Limey and which the black detective held in his hand. Malloy was remembering something Charlie Spiers had said when asked if he'd seen a knife or similar weapon on the floor of the car in which the first murder had been committed. He wondered if the conductor had just been running off at the mouth, being sarcastic.

The train's wheels, clicking against the echoing walls of the tunnel, suddenly set up a new note as though they had burst out of a cathedral or a cave. They were out in the open, in the dark meadows on the way to the yards.

10.

Charlie Spiers lived with his wife and three kids in a flat in a block of flats in Canarsie.

"They call them apartments now, but when I was a kid they called them flats," Charlie said. "I lived in Williamsburg. You know it?"

Malloy nodded. He was hunched over the kitchen table, enjoying the smell of the oilcloth on it and wondering where the hell Spiers's wife got a pattern just like the one his mother used to have on their kitchen table long, long ago. He had his overcoat on. There was a mug of coffee lost in his big hands.

"Slums. I was raised in the slums. Call them ghettos now. Black ghettos. Hispanic ghettos. Slums. I like that word better. Don't you?" Spiers went on.

Malloy nodded. He was being a listener. He looked at the

little man, still wearing his blue uniform trousers, and thought how he'd been riding the subway for twenty-five years, maybe. Down there in the middle of the roar and the clangor. Like spending a life in a tin can, filled with pebbles, getting beat on. Hard to talk above the din, even when there was a reason to talk to anybody.

Now Charlie was at home. Comfortable. Shirt off. The steam heat was banging in the radiators. A cheerful sound. His wife was in the parlor watching the television. The hum of it sounded like the murmur of a family home for the evening. Once or twice she'd peeked in to make sure the unexpected guest wasn't wanting for anything.

The kids weren't around.

"One works for Con Ed. Quiet boy. Still lives at home though he's past twenty. Reads, loves to read. Girl's going out to a movie with a friend. Right here in the neighborhood. Canarsie's a good place. Williamsburg used to be a good place. At least not so bad. Tough, but you were safe in your own neighborhood. I don't feel so safe any more. Do you?"

Malloy shook his head.

"Must have shaken you, that man being killed on your train," he said.

"Hell, I seen worse than that," Charlie boasted.

Malloy simply looked and listened as Charlie described some of the horrors and dangers he'd encountered in his years in the trenches of the city.

"Seen lots of dead ones. Seems like it's worse lately though. Last few years. Maybe the last five. I don't know. Maybe it's just you remember things different when you was young."

"You got a pretty good memory," Malloy said.

Charlie's eyes narrowed a trifle. He wasn't used to flattery. He expected it would cost him something.

"You able to picture the scenes in your head?" Malloy asked.

44

"Yeah?" Charlie was getting more suspicious.

"You able to see that guy with his hat on his chest?"

"I told you everything I knew about that."

"I know you did. But I didn't know what I was looking for then."

"Now you know?"

Malloy shook his head. "But maybe I see a glimmer of light."

"O.K. Ask me."

"You really see a card from a Monopoly game?"

"I seen it."

"What was it? I mean which one was it?"

"I can't remember a thing like that."

"Close your eyes," Malloy said. "Can you see the guy on the floor?"

Charlie closed his eyes. "Yeah," he breathed as if he were about to fall asleep.

"Which one was it?"

"Don't know."

"What color?"

"Color?"

"Yeah, I been looking at a Monopoly game. The cards got colors. Stripes of different colors at the top," Malloy explained.

"Yeah, that's right," Charlie agreed.

"So, can you see the color?"

"No color. Was one of them other cards."

Malloy waited. He allowed the image to fix itself in Charlie's head. He saw the smile forming on Charlie's lips.

"It was one of the railroads," Charlie said. He opened his eyes. "Short Line," he added triumphantly.

"A subway's a railroad. Shuttle's a short line," Malloy said.

"Ain't you hot in that overcoat?" Charlie asked.

"Christ, I don't really know any more, you know? I mean I'm down in the subway all goddamn day, popping up into

45

the cold, then down into the heat. At first I'd put it on and take it off. Pain in the ass."

He stood up.

"Your wife makes good coffee."

"Yeah," Charlie said, and got up like a good householder should to see his guest to the door. His wife, hearing the sounds of departure, came out of the parlor and stood in the doorway smiling.

"You're sure you won't have another cup of coffee? Maybe a piece of that cake, now?"

Malloy smiled and shook his head, throwing up a hand as though fending off such a wealth of hospitality.

"I hope our gabbing didn't disturb your TV," he apologized.

"I don't hardly watch it. Some things we like. 'All In The Family' was good when Edith was on it. Now it's foolish. In the bar I mean."

"Like the old 'Duffy's Tavern' on radio. You remember that?" Charlie said.

"Sure I do," Malloy said.

"Funny. Didn't seem so silly on radio," Charlie said.

"Did you really fold that man's hands that way?" Malloy asked.

"No," Charlie said. He dipped his head as though embarrassed.

"You said you did."

"No, you said it and I said that, yeah, that's the way it was. It seemed like a nice thing to do. I was sorry I hadn't thought to do it."

"I understand," Malloy said soothingly. "You know who folded his hands that way?"

"Some kid."

"Child?"

"No, I mean kid from where I'm looking. Maybe twenty-three, four or five. A little older than my oldest boy."

"Can you describe him?"

46

Charlie thought for a long moment, then shook his head.

"I know. I'll try closing my eyes, but I can tell you it won't work this time."

He closed his eyes and opened them before too long.

"I can't. You understand. The kid was—." He hesitated.

"I know. He was alive. Seems we only notice the dead any more," Malloy said.

Malloy left Canarsie and went right over to the police property office at 1 Police Plaza. Will Ory was on duty behind the counter. It was no trouble getting a look at the envelope containing the articles taken from Mrs. Spector's body. They had not yet been claimed by her relatives.

There was the usual assortment of things a woman would carry in her purse and pockets, except for a dirty, bent Monopoly card. It was for Park Place.

The killer had told the cops where he would strike next.

11.

"The police have already been here twice," Mrs. Gottlieb said, leaning forward as though ready to leap at Malloy.

Malloy sat on the edge of the chintz-covered chair, balancing a fragile cup and saucer and a wafer-thin cookie he knew was going to crumple in his fingers and mess up the rug. He hadn't wanted the tea, but Mrs. Gottlieb was a woman not used to taking no for an answer.

"I've answered these questions; we've answered these questions," she quickly amended, casting a sidelong glance at Mrs. Roth, "three times in all."

The quiet Mrs. Roth laughed softly.

"Yes, Rose?" Mrs. Gottlieb said, turning on her friend.

"Nothing, Myrna. What you said. It was just like a scene on television."

"Nevertheless true. Now why do you have to know all the same things?" she challenged Malloy again.

He wanted a hand free for his reply, and didn't know what to do with the cookie, so he dropped it in his tea. He pulled down the lower lid of first one eye, then the other.

"Some people see with this eye, other people see with this eye."

"A philosopher we've got here." Mrs. Gottlieb smiled.

It was a sweetly sarcastic remark, but one that settled any differences between them.

"Ask," she said.

"You were sitting beside Mrs. Spector?" Malloy began.

"Next but one," Mrs. Gottlieb answered a trifle regretfully.

"I was sitting next to Sadie," Mrs. Roth nearly whispered.

It wasn't that Mrs. Gottlieb wanted to steal any limelight. What glory could be gathered from such a tragic event? It was just that Rose was not the most observant of women.

"Tell him when you first thought something was funny," Mrs. Gottlieb said.

"What do you mean, 'funny'?"

"You know."

Mrs. Roth colored slightly.

"It was just a comment I made, Myrna, not an observation," Mrs. Roth demurred.

"What was that?" Malloy prompted her gently.

"Sadie talked to the boy, then she blushed."

"Do you think he insulted her?" Malloy asked.

"What?" Mrs. Roth said as though he'd awakened her.

"Did the boy say something improper?"

"I don't think so. I couldn't hear too clearly, but I don't think so. He had that kind of voice."

"What kind of voice is that?"

"Soft. Romantic. You know?"

Malloy nodded, but he didn't know.

My God, he thought, middle-aged ladies who blush at the

49

sound of a young man's voice. Middle-aged ladies who blush telling about it. Innocent women in this day and age.

"Then you didn't actually hear any of his words?"

"No."

Mrs. Gottlieb let out a small sigh as though to remark upon her friend's lack of attention.

"How about your friend's words? Did you hear what she said to him?"

"Not really. I wasn't trying to listen, you understand?"

"You don't suppose she insulted him in some way?"

"How could she do that?" Mrs. Roth asked, genuinely puzzled.

"He might have been crowding her. She might have asked him nicely to give her a little more room."

"It didn't look like that to me."

"He might have touched her. Things like that happen."

"She wasn't blushing from anger or embarrassment," Mrs. Roth said. "It was nothing like that. Just she was pleased. He was a nice young man. Maybe she was thinking her son would be about his age if she and Herb had had any children."

"She talked to him and then what?"

"She talked to him twice," Mrs. Gottlieb said.

"That's right," Mrs. Roth agreed.

"Then what?"

"She made some remark to me. She leaned across Rose and made some remark to me about the play," Mrs. Gottlieb said.

"You've got it wrong, Myrna. Sadie spoke to you, then she turned back to the boy. Then she leaned up against me."

Suddenly Rose looked straight into Malloy's eyes. Hers were terrified. She knew that her friend had been dead at that moment, but she'd been all unaware of it. She'd been chattering on with Myrna and the rest about a stupid play and her friend had been dead.

"The young man. Where was he at that moment?"

"When she leaned against me?"

"Yes."

"Sitting right there. A second later he got up. The train was pulling into Grand Central."

Mrs. Roth's hands started to tremble. She looked down at them as though wondering what they were doing. Mrs. Gottlieb caught her friend's hands in her own.

"We've answered all these questions," she said again, angry now.

"Just a few more," Malloy murmured softly, not liking any of it, but going on all the same. "Please."

"Sadie fell to one side when the train stopped. She tipped over, then fell off the seat onto the floor," Mrs. Roth went on.

There was the sound of rising agitation in her voice. Her eyes were wider than ever, and still stared at Malloy.

"So, a young man coming onto the train saw that we were in trouble," Mrs. Gottlieb broke in forcefully. "He asked me to help him. We picked Sadie up, one under each arm. I didn't know she was dead then. Not then."

"It was the same one," Mrs. Roth whispered.

"This young man and I laid Sadie out on the bench. I thought she'd fainted. The young man put Sadie's purse under her head," Mrs. Gottlieb rattled on.

"The same one," Mrs. Roth said again.

"After a little while I could tell Sadie was . . . oh!" Mrs. Gottlieb finished, and finally let it register that her friend, Rose, had said the same thing twice.

"The boy who got back on the train and helped put Sadie on the bench was the same one who sat next to her. Only he'd taken his scarf off," Mrs. Roth said in horror.

The madness of it was more than she could manage any longer and she began to cry.

12.

Dr. John Mercado had a string of degrees that he told on his fingers like the prayer beads in the hands of a nun. How he'd ever ended up as the chief psychiatrist of New York County was anybody's guess. He would have more properly been sheltered in a set of ivy-covered walls.

He was of an indeterminate age, probably well past retirement by any reasonable standards. No one knew for sure. Once a chief of detectives had been interested enough to pull Mercado's file. The space to be filled in with his age had been blotted out. Mercado promised to fill out a new form, but never did. He looked to be anywhere from fifty-two to eighty-five depending upon how snow-white hair and skin as translucent as pink alabaster struck you. The hair began halfway back on his shining skull, then fell to his shoulders in a graceful cascade. He had a disconcerting habit of picking his nose. He did it delicately, and never produced any debris. Still it wasn't in keeping with his professorial appearance and saintly bearing.

He did not enter a room, but blessed it.

When he spoke, his voice had the thunderous, if muted, quality one would expect from God or, at least, Charlton Heston playing God.

He had a smile like a baby's.

"Let me tell you what I like about my job. I get to play God. I get to decide whether some human being, at the end of his rope, knew what he was doing when he bashed in his grandmother's head with a poker. I get to decide whether some woman knew it was wrong to stick a knife into some brute of a husband who'd infected her with a venereal disease he'd picked up from some prostitute in a saloon.

"Want to know what I don't like? The McNaughton rule. Does the perpetrator know right from wrong? Not now, not at some time in the past, but at the moment when the crime was committed.

"Take murder. Any decent, halfway civilized human being knows that you'd have to be crazy to take another person's life outside of war or self-defense. Psychiatrists would agree. One of the few times when professionals agree with laymen. If the perpetrators of such crimes are crazy, they cannot be brought to trial. They must have been crazy to have murdered. Right? Not according to McNaughton. They can now be adjudged unmad.

"Unmad is a word of my own devising, conceived out of a need for clarity. They are not sane, you understand, merely unmad.

"Whittlesey, are you following me?"

"I'm just a poor, dumb nigger," Limey said.

"Don't shuck with me," Mercado said.

"Don't try to confuse me, I beg you," Limey replied.

Mercado grinned and picked his nose.

He assigned other psychiatrists to do the work. He sat

around the homicide division offices in Manhattan South, at the Thirteenth Precinct on 21st Street, or in the offices of the Medical Examiner on First Avenue.

He liked cops.

"If there was any reason why the average cop couldn't have a license to carry a gun, the son of a bitch would be on the other side of the law. For the gun is his cock, and his cock is his manhood, and his manhood gives him a place in a world otherwise hostile to bullies."

This was one of the many maxims with which he regaled them. He was a brutal critic of official behavior.

He was also intelligent, gentle, perceptive, cooperative, and generous. Also a homicide groupie.

He wanted to help Gertie and Limey with their case of casual murder.

"Three screwball cases," Gertie said. "More, but we got reasons for the other fourteen subway deaths since that first one got laid out by the killer."

"Which killer is that?" Mercado asked.

"The Monopoly Killer," Gertie said. "Oh, damn. There I go saying it and Seagrave ain't even tagged the killings like that in his columns yet."

"He will soon enough if he finds out that conductor saw one of those cards and that another was found in Mrs. Spector's coat pocket," Limey said.

"You sure that's all the Monopoly cards this knifer's spread around? You checked all the subway homicides?" Posner asked.

"We could have missed one if it was on the floor of the train or the station, but I checked all the property envelopes myself and these three are the only ones. Besides we got reasons for the other fourteen subway killings."

"Hey, Gertie," Malloy said.

He was sitting a little apart from the others who were more or less grouped around the Chief of Detectives, Homi-

54

cide, Randolph "Rank" Posner. It seemed as though Malloy sat in the one half shadow in the otherwise brightly lit room. It was his natural habitat and, hands in pocket, leaning forward, his natural pose. Like an animal peering warily out of the dark of its cave.

"What reason do you have, Gertie, for the kid somebody shoved under the A train? What motive you got for the drunk beaten to death at Fulton Street station?" Malloy said.

Gertie looked at Malloy as though he'd just spit on the rug.

"What's eating you? You know damn well what I mean. Those casual homicides is understandable casual homicides. They ain't a series of killings done by a super-nut."

Malloy leaned back in his chair, closed his eyes, and waved his hand as if he were saying goodbye.

"You got a wild hair?" Gertie asked. "That emergency nurse leave you hanging?"

Malloy opened his eyes. There was a warning in them.

"Let me profile this pious killer. Let me try," Mercado said softly.

Mercado played with the fingers of his hand, telling his degrees. Taking comfort from the fact that he was a learned man and knew practically nothing. Still, what little he knew might mean something.

"What do we have? This killer is most probably a young man. That isn't conjecture but presumable fact based upon the two accounts. That of the death of the businessman."

He looked at Gertie.

"Mr. Howard Morrison," Gertie said.

Malloy's head came up sharply at the sound of the name. He looked startled, then sad as though he'd just been told of the death of someone he'd known.

"Mr. Morrison and Mrs. Spector," Mercado went on. "The conductor told Malloy the young man who so reverently folded the dead man's hands on his chest—"

"Stomach," Malloy interrupted.

"What?" Mercado said sharply, caught short in mid-lecture.

"Stomach. Hands folded on his stomach."

"Who gives a damn?" Gertie said belligerently, wanting everybody to know that he hadn't been cowed by Malloy's sharp warning glance when he'd mentioned Irma Sweet.

"It could mean something to Dr. Mercado's analysis."

"That's right, Gertie," Mercado said. "Don't be an asshole. Shut up and let me finish this."

Posner grunted his agreement.

"I'm not sure it does make much difference in how we view the detail," Mercado said. "People were laid out with hands, one on top of the other, on the breast in the old days. In the last twenty years the mode has been more informal, hands lightly clasped in a more comfortable, casual arrangement on the abdomen."

He flashed a sudden grin, amused at what he, himself, had just said.

"Got to keep them comfortable, even in their coffins, right?"

"And casual," Malloy added.

"What I'm getting at is this," Mercado went on, serious again. "This killer is following a ritual. He doesn't want his killings to seem brutal and unfeeling. They have symbolic value to him. They have purpose."

He held up a finger.

"The murders are committed in the midst of crowds. That may have symbolic value to him as well. The danger of overpopulation. Being 'lost in the crowd.' Having anonymity in a crowd. More important, being forced to be faceless in the crowd."

"Thumbing his nose at the crowd," Malloy said.

"That too. Classically, assassins are described as lurking in the shadows, catching their victims alone, isolated from their fellows. This killer sees the far greater isolation imposed upon each one of us by the congestion of the great cities. We are afraid to look at one another on the street, in the restaurants, and, certainly, in any space so closely confined that recognition of another's humanity might be a challenge and an invitation to dispute and violence. This young man sees very clearly that there is no longer any safety in numbers. He is saying, 'In the mob lurks death, silent and faceless.' "

"The game cards?"

"The obvious interpretation comes readily enough. He wants to leave his mark on a society that ignores him as it ignores most of us. He wants to play games with it and us. To flaunt the audacity of his crimes. To tear apart any complacency we may have left to us. He is saying that we are all victims of the throw of the dice, the turn of a card. Success and fame, power, riches, and the love of women are no more than the product of blind luck."

"Bullshit," Gertie murmured.

"Exactly," Mercado agreed.

"By the way," Limey said casually, "the eyewitnesses who ran the killer off before he could lay Philo Lincoln out the way he likes to do disagree on a description. Age, height, color, and nearly everything."

"But more say young than not," Posner said. The consensus was that they would have to go with that.

13.

When he was in the mood, Linus sought the streets and the open air. The weather didn't matter to him. It was his state of mind that made the difference. If he was particularly mellow he went to Central Park and sat on the benches on the path that led to the entrance to the zoo, or sought the quiet shadows of the Cloisters in Fort Tryon Park, or sat on the steps looking at the lions, Patience and Fortitude, that guarded the New York Public Library.

If he was feeling mean he sought the shopping streets, Fifth and Madison, 42nd and 34th, and played bumper cars with the pedestrians. With a fixed, manic grin on his boyish face, he picked a path right down the center of the crowd, ducking the very big men, slamming his hip or knee into women and children, shouldering old ladies out of the way, sometimes knocking their packages out of their hands and making a great dumb show about helping them retrieve them. On occasion he even tested himself on men as big as himself and bigger, daring them with his eyes to protest. There was something in his stare recognizably mad and there had never been any takers.

"Bam! Bam! Bam!" he murmured to himself as he elbowed his way through the crowds.

He crossed the streets against the lights and traffic, sidestepping the bumpers gracefully, laughing into the faces of the cursing drivers as he reached the other side.

He made noises like a marching band.

"Boom! Boom! Boom!"

He pursed his lips and tootled like a bugle, fluttered like a trombone, made big wet sounds like a tuba.

"Ping! Ping-a-dee-ping!" he clucked as he held up his arm as though leaning against the weight of a glockenspiel, his other hand hammering away at the invisible bars of chrome-plate with an invisible hammer.

Those who smiled at such nonsense smiled warily. Linus always looked as though he were about to kill when he marched down the avenue.

He was the master of his parade.

When he'd been a small boy, off to watch a parade for the first time, in the keeping of yet another man who was supposed to act the father to him, he'd been more excited, more cheered by the display than he could ever remember having been before.

The flags whipping in the breeze, the short white tasseled boots of the majorettes, the feathers and the plumes, the clowns tumbling along the asphalt, all were a wonder. At least those snatches that Linus could see. The man he was with couldn't be bothered lifting him on his shoulder, handling him above the heads of the crowd so that Linus could have a better view.

There was a mounted policeman sitting on his chestnut horse right there at the edge of the curb. Horse and rider

59

grew still as statues as the sounds of an approaching marching band filled the air. Little Linus knew he wanted a look at this newest wonder, so he just crawled underneath the horse, braving its hooves. He could look out past the animal's front legs as the drum major came high-stepping along, the American flag carried by the color guard coming right after.

At first Linus had no idea what the warm wetness on his back and neck might be. He could see men in uniform saluting the flag from the other side of the street, and men with their hats held at their chests. The laughter made him take notice. He craned his head around and saw the horse was raining piss on him.

His foster father grabbed him by an arm, his face as red with laughter as the rest, remarking that he had heard about kids "too dumb to get in out of the rain, but never too damn dumb to come in out of the horse piss."

When the mood struck him, Linus made his own parade. But usually he liked the subways and the tunnels, the maze and tangle of them, where he could spy on the world if he chose to, or speak, or hide away forever.

A squad car slowed down along the avenue, the cops watching him like hawks. They were figuring what to do with a screwball making his own parade.

Linus cut over 42nd to Sixth and popped down the stairs to the station there.

He made his way to the IRT Lexington and rode the 6 to the 86th Street Station, where he put on his schoolboy act.

Five years before, hung over and tapped out, he'd first tried the beggar's pitch in the same spot and scored six bucks and change in a little over an hour. Then a shopping bag lady who called herself Mumblety Peg had tapped him on the elbow, pointed out the plainclothes cop who was looking him over, and invited him down into the tunnels for a pot-luck supper.

He'd never left.

14.

Honker Levine was called in to be interviewed by Rank Posner.

"We got uniforms riding the subways," he said.

"Yes, sir."

"We got plain clothes riding them, too."

"Yes, sir."

"We don't know but what the regular riders don't recognize the one just as easy as they do the other."

Honker nodded.

"We're going to beef up the detail. Everyone wears civvies."

It wasn't quite being a detective, Honker thought, but it would do for now.

"I'm putting you in charge of the extra uniforms I'm pulling in for this job. It's a chance for you."

"I appreciate that, sir."

"Sure you do. You read the papers?"

"Yes, sir."

"Well, I'm going to tell you something that isn't in the papers. This nut is dropping Monopoly cards on the bodies. The last one was for Oriental Avenue."

"There's no such street in any of the boroughs that I know of," Honker said. "I'm certain there isn't any subway station with that name."

"That's right, but there's a Chinatown," Posner said. "Now, you go arrange a duty roster for your specials with the detective in charge."

"Who would that be, sir?"

"Detective Walsh." Posner grinned. "Don't let his growling fool you. Gertie's a kidder, but he don't mean any real harm. He's the one named you for the assignment."

Honker didn't thank Gertie when he reported to him. He had the feeling it would annoy the Irishman.

"This sonofabitch likes a crowd when he slips in the knife," Gertie said. "We've got extra men, but we haven't got a fucking army. I'm going heavy during the rush hours."

Malloy coughed and Gertie looked at him sharply, as though he suspected Malloy was laughing at him again.

"Jesus Christ, I got a dry cough," Malloy said in self-defense.

"You ought to get out in the fresh air more," Gertie advised. "We'll be thinner during the small hours, but the men will be able to see down the length of the cars easier. They can walk on through easier, too. I don't want to catch anybody sleeping on this one. Stay on your feet and walking."

"Like cops on the beat," Malloy said.

"Stay out of this, Malloy. You're in here on a courtesy pass."

"Do what you want," Malloy said. He got up and left the room.

62

"Ah, hell," Gertie said. "I guess he's right. Walk some, but sit down some, too."

The first shift went out to ride the subways.

Honker took the rush hour for himself. That's when the killer struck, and Honker wanted to be there if it happened. He wanted to be in on the arrest. It was the way to a citation. Maybe a promotion and maybe a raise. He could get his nose fixed that much sooner.

15.

Linus boarded the D train at Grand Street going uptown. It was about four o'clock in the morning. There was nobody in the car. He sat for a while, rocking with the motion of the train, half dozing. There was a spot of pain as big as a quarter right in the center of his forehead, between the eyes. It felt as though he had been shot.

He got up and walked along the length of the car. He opened the end door and stepped out. The rush of air and sound pushed him back for a moment, but he leaned forward and opened the door into the next car. The lights dimmed and the car was dark as they lost power for a second, then they brightened again.

There was an old Chinese man sitting facing him about halfway up the aisle.

They looked at each other like old enemies.

Linus went down and sat on a side bench. He stared at

the old man, whose eyes were like chips of black stone. He looked back at Linus without blinking, his face never moved, but Linus thought a ghost of a smile passed across the dry, ancient lips. The Oriental looked away, staring straight ahead, patient and quiet within himself.

Linus got up and moved to the short bench that faced the old man. He was riding backwards. Their knees were almost touching. The old man looked at Linus again. They stared at each other. Then the Chinese looked away and sighed.

Linus moved again. He leaned forward, lifting himself off the seat, turning around, and settling himself heavily, thrusting his elbow into the old man's side. The man grunted softly. Linus smiled and thrust his face up close to the other man's. His hand slipped out of the pocket of his sweater.

"Did you tell me to move, mister? Is that what you asked me to do?" Linus inquired with mock courtesy.

He tensed himself to stab with the knife. He felt a sharp blow between his ribs. It knocked him sideways and took the breath out of him. The old man was on his feet and moving away, his hands weaving small circles in front of his chest. Linus leaped on him. Again he felt the sharp wedge of the old man's fingers piercing his side, but the Chinese stumbled back and put one hand to his own ribs. When he took it away there was blood on it. His expression scarcely changed.

He retreated two more steps and planted his feet in a classic pose of Oriental defense. His hands and forearms were up again, weaving in the air. Long ago, when he'd been a young man, he'd been a soldier in the most successful of the Tongs. He knew that he was in a fight for his life once more.

It saddened, but did not surprise, him.

The car slammed against the side rails. Linus and the old man faced each other. Linus was no longer so arrogantly sure of himself. He thrust out with the knife, but he had

65

not committed himself to taking a step in close enough, and the Chinese avoided it with ease.

Linus began to stalk him, shifting the blade from hand to hand the way he'd been taught by gutter toughs when he was a kid. He feinted with the left. Before he could pass the knife, or withdraw the hand, the old man had chopped down with the side of his hand at the base of Linus's thumb. A slash of pain ran up his arm to his collarbone. The knife clattered to the floor.

The Chinese went for it with a long swooping motion. The years had stiffened his back and made him slow. Linus kicked him in the throat. The old man went over on his back. Linus was on him, the knife in his hand again. He lifted it and struck down. The old man grasped his wrist in both hands and held the blow away from his chest. He kicked and they rolled over. Linus gasped. He felt something wet and warm as he touched his side. His own blood.

Suddenly he was afraid and angrier than he had ever been. The old man was on his feet, watching him like a snake, his eyes still expressionless. Linus rushed at him with the knife held low. He screamed as loudly as he could. It scarcely rose above the scream of steel wheels on steel rails. He powered the knife right through the old man's defending forearms. He felt it enter flesh.

The train roared into Broadway-Lafayette.

The old man's eyes filled with tears. His life was leaking out of his eyes. His mouth screwed up in pain. There was no reason to be stoic any more.

Linus knew the old man was dead, although he clung to the pole and would not fall. He slipped a card into the pocket of his overcoat. The doors opened and he left the train. He turned to watch as the doors closed and the train jolted into motion.

The Chinese fell as the train picked up speed.

Malloy was the first man at the scene when the alarm went out.

16.

"What were you doing riding the trains at that hour?" Irma said. Her voice was strained. It sounded as though it were about to break in half like a bundle of straw.

"That's what Gertie asked me," Malloy said.

"So what did you answer him?"

"I told him to go to hell," Malloy said evenly.

She stared at him hard, tears filling up in her eyes. She took a bite of her Chinese food as though doubting she could swallow it.

"Good goddamn," she said, "this crap is loaded with MSG. Didn't you tell the waiter we didn't want any goddamn MSG?"

"You heard me tell him," Malloy said softly.

"Stuff will kill you. Rot your kidneys."

A tear dropped into the middle of her plate of Lemon Chicken. Malloy reached over and placed his big hand on top of hers.

"Christ, I didn't mean that *you* should go to hell, Irma. I'm not mad at you."

"That's good to know," she said, not much mollified.

"I'm still a little ticked off at Gertie. He was making out like he thought *I* could be the sonofabitch doing these knifings."

"What?"

Two bright circles of color appeared as if by magic on Irma's cheeks. She was hopping mad in the flick of an eyelash.

"Where the hell does that bastard get off—" she started to rage.

"Hey, hey, hey," Malloy soothed. "He doesn't really think that. He was just putting me on. He was just insulting me to get my goat."

"And he got it?"

"I guess."

She took another bite of the chicken.

"It was a Chinese he stabbed this time?" she asked.

"That's right. A merchant from Pell Street."

Irma put down her chopsticks.

"I'm not hungry, Malloy," she said.

"Me neither."

He threw down a couple of bills for the meal. Irma slipped out of the booth. He helped her into her chubby fur. She walked out in front of him.

"Hey, Irma," he said, "you got the sweetest little ass."

They went back to her place and made love, quietly and gently. It wasn't wild and passionate, but that was all right.

Later on Irma cried some. That was all right too.

When he was asleep, rolling over to find the edge of the bed, she lay on her back and stared at the patterns made by the street light as it shone through the slats of the blinds onto the ceiling. Blinds were practical matters in a Manhattan efficiency apartment.

The patterns thrown onto the ceiling of her childhood bedroom in the small house in a small town back in Ohio were filtered through ruffled curtains, and the source of the illumination had been the moon.

What she remembered best of those years was the pervasive aura of delicate silence in all the rooms, the gentle gloom made up of mauve shadows. The furniture in the parlor had always been covered with white sheets against the dust. The drapes had been drawn. The room waited for her mother to get well.

She did rise from her sick bed from time to time, but the intervals never seemed long enough for the family or the house to take up a normal tempo of life. Something would happen and her mother would take to bed again. It was a disorder of the heart, real but elusive.

Her father had been the quietest of men. She could never remember his raising his voice much above a murmur. He was the manager of one of the town's two shoe stores. He'd had opportunities to buy out the shop, her mother told her, but he never had the ambition for advancement or the will for responsibility.

Her mother informed Irma, a hundred times a day, of her father's failings. The litany was delivered in a thin, whining voice that took on the force of hammer blows unless one learned to shut it out.

Irma never talked much to her father. He came home from work, prepared the meal, even when Irma was grown, went in to see her mother for a brief visit, from which he always emerged looking patient and sad, sat down in his easy chair placed near the stove in the kitchen, and read the paper.

Later he would take a book upstairs to his own room, which was very small, having been the box room not much bigger than a closet.

Irma had been the nurse. Dr. Pastor often patted her hand

69

and said that she'd been born to it. Irma believed him. At least she said she did when she realized that her mother would object strongly, would develop a much-worsened condition when the matter of Irma's going off to school was raised, unless she declared her intention of becoming a nurse. Somehow her mother was afraid to stand in the way of such a selfless desire. Perhaps she expected that Irma would return after graduation better able to see to her comfort.

Irma did return, because her father unexpectedly died first.

When she cried at his funeral her mother berated her for it, saying that it was time she knew her father had been a philanderer, had kept a mistress in the next town for the last twenty years. That made Irma feel happier for him.

It was also enough to make Irma believe she could break off the vicious cycle of service and dependency into which she and her mother had fallen. In the end it hadn't worked out that way at all, of course. Irma did go to New York and got the job at Bellevue, but it wasn't very long before her mother was with her again. She shared an apartment grown too small with a mother who never ceased complaining about the city and regretting the good life in Ohio she'd left behind.

In the end Irma's sacrifice became her mother's sacrifice. Then the mother died, and things were not much better, or even much different somehow, until Malloy came along.

His legs jerked out violently in his sleep. She heard the painful closing of his throat as he caught the nightmare's protesting scream. She knew the moment when his eyes flew open. He crept out of the bed and went into the bathroom to quietly wash his face.

Now he would dress and go out to prowl the subways, looking for some answer necessary to him in the mouth of every tunnel, just as she looked for some answer necessary to her in the face of every old shopping bag lady that came, wounded, into emergency.

She closed her eyes when he bent over to peer into her face. He hated to think that she could not sleep.

17.

"What are you thinking, Ira?" his wife asked Honker at the breakfast table.

"Huh?" he replied, lifting his head sharply.

"That's brilliant," Marsha said. "What were you doing with your nose practically in the cereal? You see a bug? It's no bug, I assure you, it's a raisin."

"I was thinking about Malloy."

"Is that another Irish cop who makes fun of your beautiful nose?"

"He works for Transit. He used to be a cop, though, before he took four in the belly."

Marsha gave a little scream. "Bite your tongue. I don't want to hear about four of whatever, wherever."

"He knows the subway system like I know the curls on

your bickie," Honker said. "He could be the rabbi for every motorman ever drives a train. There are nooks and crannies maybe only Malloy knows. Malloy and the people who live in the tunnels."

"So what are you thinking about him?" Marsha asked as Honker started thinking about Malloy again.

"Not only does Malloy know the system that good, but I think he's got like a sixth sense about it."

Marsha was interested now. She was a graduate of Hunter in psychology and sociology. She believed in Jehovah and holistic medicine. She had faith in Transcendental Meditation and ESP.

"How do you mean that?" she asked, her elbows propped up on the kitchen table.

"Detective Walsh, and everyone else, figured this Monopoly Killer would always make his move in crowds. We're riding the trains in big numbers at the rush hours. When things get slow there's not so many of us riding.

"Except Malloy. Malloy is riding through Chinatown at four o'clock in the morning on an empty train."

"Not empty," Marsha said.

"Empty except for him, an old storekeeper, and the killer."

"But you said he didn't see the killer. He only saw the old man after he was dead. That's not doing so good."

"I didn't say he was lucky."

"That's not being so smart, either."

"I didn't say he was smart. I just said he had a nose."

"You got a nose," Marsha said.

Honker touched it.

"Marsha," he said as though she'd meant to insult him.

Marsha shook her head impatiently, but fondly. She was as ambitious for her husband as he was for himself.

"I'm saying you smelled out the fact that Malloy works on hunches and instincts. I'm just saying that maybe you can't figure what a killer's going to do, but some people can feel what he's going to do."

"Malloy."

"Malloy's going to find that killer," Marsha predicted.

"I'm going to be there when he does," Honker finished.

18.

Seagrave draped himself over the counter of the property clerk. He was chronically tired, but preferred to suffer it rather than waste his time sleeping.

"You look like you're about to pass out on your feet," Will Ory advised him.

"I'm doing all right," Seagrave said. "I'm like an old fighter, you know? I mean I take every chance I can get to hang on and rest. That's why I can go fifteen every day."

Ory shook his head. He was an old cop. He couldn't understand why anybody wouldn't take every opportunity to have forty winks. He was sitting in a chair now, his feet planted far apart as though he feared someone might want to tip him over. His gut hung over his belt like a load of wash.

"I hear how you live," he said. "All that loving's no good for you."

"That's what my old grandmother used to tell me," Seagrave grinned. "Now let me ask you."

"I'm listening," Ory said, when Seagrave didn't go on.

"What would you like to know?" Seagrave asked.

"What can I do for you?"

"Well, there is a small favor I could ask."

"Go ahead, ask it."

"Can I have a look at the stuff found on the body of that Chinaman killed on Sixth Avenue?"

"Oh my, oh my," Ory said.

"What's the matter?"

"I got my orders on that stuff."

"Like what orders?"

"Like not to show it to any unauthorized persons."

"Is that how you think of me?" Seagrave said as though Ory had struck him right where he lived.

"Well, no," Ory said doubtfully, not being sure just how he did think of Seagrave.

"I thought we were friends," Seagrave said mournfully.

"We are."

"Christ, just a glance. A glimpse. A little peek no bigger than a gnat's ass."

Ory wavered.

"I mean, hell Ory, you asked me was there anything you could do for me."

Ory thought about that. Seagrave was right; he had asked if Seagrave needed anything. He went over to the pigeon holes and bins. He removed the manila envelope and brought it back to the counter.

Seagrave reached for it. Ory snatched it back.

"Just a peek, goddammit." Ory had the suspicion he was somehow being conned, but he couldn't put his finger on the switch.

Ory spread out the material in the envelope, then started putting it back piece by piece. There was nothing much. The old man had known better than to carry any valuables with him on his underground travels. Ory lifted a silk handkerchief. A square of cardboard fell onto the counter top. He picked it up and tucked it into the envelope, but not before Seagrave saw it was a Monopoly property card for Boardwalk.

Ory spread the little metal clasp and held the envelope in his two hands. Seagrave slipped a folded twenty between them.

"Is that a bribe?" Ory asked.

"Go get yourself some lovin'," Seagrave said.

He went right on back and wrote his column in his cubicle of an office just off the press room. He enumerated the killings that might be laid at the feet of this single subway killer. There had been at least four in the last ten days. He gave the case a name. "The Monopoly Killings" was in his column, "City Shadows," out on the streets, becoming part of the history of the metropolis, by nightfall.

Seagrave went out to check the action. He enjoyed the glitter and swank around Rockefeller Center, bought himself a drink in one of the posh bars.

A girl with eyes the color of smoke sat down on the stool next to him and let him feel the pressure of her thigh.

"Are you buying me one, Seagrave?" she asked.

"Now, Sally, you know you don't drink, and I know that you don't drink."

"Slow night," the streetwalker said. "Just keeping in practice. How about a lot of funny for a little money?"

"Cutting your rates?"

"Just for you."

"How come?"

"You've got a reputation, Seagrave. Big swordsman around the boroughs."

Seagrave laughed and cooled his lips on the ice in his glass.

"What do you say?" Sally urged.

"Now, I know that I don't pay, and you know that I don't pay . . ." Seagrave started to say.

Sally leaned over, pouting her lips, and gave him a quick kiss on the mouth to shut him up.

"You as powerful as they say?" she asked.

"To what particular power do you refer?"

"Oh, that, sure," she said grabbing at his crotch for a flip moment. "Power with the people."

"Which people?"

"Big people. Movie producers, model agents, the talent scouts for *Penthouse* and *Hustler*."

"I know a few," Seagrave smiled.

"Can you do me any good?"

"Not a scrap. They've all got their own fish to fry."

"That's no way to seduce a girl."

"I only print the truth."

She hauled at his elbow as she got off the stool, showing a lot of leg in the doing.

"Come on, then, you sweet-talking son of a bitch."

"What's this?" Seagrave exclaimed in mock surprise. "Giving away samples?"

"Just want to try you out, Seagrave. Even a working girl gets curious about a man with a big reputation."

He resisted the pull of her hands. He shook his head and laughed.

"It'll cost you," he said.

There was a little chill in her eyes as she regarded him carefully. Hookers worked on half a dozen psychological levels at the same time, hard as nails at one end of the emotional spectrum, fragile as crystal at the other.

She didn't like what she saw. Something puzzled her. She didn't want to spend any time on it.

"Hey, you really are the big gun, aren't you?"

He shrugged, too modest to say his reputation was well-deserved.

Sally looked into his face a moment longer, then turned away.

"Screw yourself," she called back gaily over her shoulder, loud enough for the entire bar to hear.

Seagrave bought himself another.

19.

Old Mumblety Peg squatted on her haunches and lifted the
bandages that were taped to Linus's side. They were clean
enough. She'd made them from one of the many cast-off
slips and petticoats she wore underneath her three skirts.
She pursed her lips and made a noise.

"Do you know what you're doing?" Linus asked.

She put the palm of her hand on his forehead.

"You got a fever," she announced.

"How does the cut look?" Linus asked.

"That adhesive tape won't keep it closed. I didn't think
it would. Needs stitches."

"What do you know about it?" Linus demanded harshly.

She looked at him carefully, sizing him up.

"I didn't ask to do you no favors," she said evenly.

"I mean, do you know what you're doing?"

Her eyes grew thoughtful. She lifted her head as though listening to something far away.

"I used to be a nurse," she said.

"A real nurse?"

"What they call a practical nurse. But I was licensed and everything."

"Can you sew me up?" Linus asked.

Peg shuffled back. She stood up with great effort, her legs stiff and unresponsive. She staggered up against the wall of the tunnel.

"What a thing to ask."

"Well, can you?"

"Why don't you just go to the hospital? They'll fix you right up."

"They'll want to know how I got cut."

"How did you get cut?"

"I told you. I told you," Linus said impatiently, his voice rising dangerously.

"All right," Peg soothed. "Just asked. All I did was ask."

"Two Spics jumped me when I was working the dodge at Fulton Street."

"What'd they get?"

"I told you. Three dollars and change."

She thought about that and smiled. Her head didn't match things up the right way. Sometimes she was as bright as a penny. Sometimes she was somewhere else.

"Can you fix me up, Peg?" Linus asked softly. "Can you do that for me?"

"It'll cost you," she said shrewdly.

"I know. How much?"

"Three Monopoly games—no—four Monopoly games and two games of Parchesi."

"Whatever you say," Linus agreed.

"You wait here," Peg said and went shuffling off down the steam tunnel in her pair of old men's shoes with the broken backs.

Linus lay up against the tunnel wall. He'd been stupid taking on the old man. There'd been something about the old Chink's eyes that should have told him he was no easy mark. Besides, in the empty car there'd been too much room for his victim to maneuver, to get away from the knife. The old man had made Linus cut himself. With his own knife. He'd been strong for his age and build.

Linus closed his eyes. He was very tired. Feverish. Why had he changed his way of doing things? Did he really want to get caught? Is that why he was dropping those Monopoly cards on the bodies? Did he want somebody to get into the game with him? This big game he was playing. Did he need his life at stake to make the game worth playing?

The coin of pain between his eyes made him feel faint. It was almost worse than the burning hurt in his side.

He heard a sound like the squeaking of rats. He held his breath and listened for the sound of their tiny nails. He peered down the corridor. The squeaking grew louder, rhythmic and monotonous. He saw a shape looming up out of the shadows.

The wheelchair was old, made of wood, probably even worth something as an antique. Linus knew it had a broken wicker seat, repaired with string. The man who pushed it, and all his belongings piled in it, was called Eddie B. The initial might have served for a last name, but he was never called simply Eddie, always Eddie B.

Linus winced against the protest of the wheels. He opened his mouth, ready to scream. Eddie B came to a halt.

"How you doing, Linus?" he asked.

"Go away. I've got no time," Linus said.

"Time for what?"

"Time to talk."

"All right," Eddie B said and, removing his belongings from the seat of the wheelchair, made himself comfortable in it, settling down as though prepared to stay some long while.

82

"I said I don't want any company," Linus grated.

"I came to see Mumblety Peg," Eddie B said reasonably.

Linus shivered and hugged himself with his arms. He'd forgotten to feed the locker at Penn Station. They were cleaned at intervals, the goods inside taken off for later sale. He'd lost his mac.

"You should dress warmer," Eddie B said.

Linus felt a pinpoint of rage growing inside his chest.

"You want to borrow this blanket I got here?" Eddie B asked.

"Go away," Linus said. "Go away!" he shouted, and started to rise up in anger. The pain caused by the action slammed him back against the wall, breathless, weak as a kitten.

Peg came back, a busted tennis racket in her hand.

"You see these strings?" she said as she set a can of water on to boil. "Catgut. Ain't really a cat's guts." She laughed as though mad. "Catgut," she said again, enjoying the sound of it.

She cut off a strand of it, threw it into her coffee water to kill the germs and make it pliable. She took a hooked needle of the sort used for trussing up chickens from the lapel of her jacket, where a collection of pins and needles was lined up, and dropped that into the water too.

She squatted over the can, waiting for the water to boil, her lips pursed and whistling a soundless tune. Eddie B stared.

Linus shivered. He didn't like the idea of her old hands touching him, but he hesitated about going to a hospital. He may have bled some in the subway car. The cops in their laboratories might have already typed some and, seeing that it was different from that of the dead man, would be on the lookout for anybody with an unexplained wound.

The water hadn't really come to a good rolling boil when Peg fished the gut and needle out of it. She split the strand with a dirty thumbnail, then split it again. She threaded the needle with a thread of it. Eddie B was beside himself with the wonder of it. Something spoke to Peg. She lifted her head, nodded and fished in her pocket. She washed her hands in the can with a piece of soap. She dried them on her apron and then by waving them in the air. There was a clean smell in the air and that made Linus feel better.

Peg took the bandage away from the wound. The lips of it were serrated and puckered, marked with little scabs and glistening pockets of raw flesh. She wiped it clean with a piece of rag dipped in the can.

Then she got on her knees and bent over the young man's body. Her old fingers became surprisingly deft. They gathered up the edges of the wound and held them together while she took a stitch through the flesh.

Linus winced and bit his lip, but he didn't cry out. He stared at her old head as though wondering if she wasn't causing him unnecessary pain on purpose. Or, rather, for some hidden purpose of her own.

The needle bit into his flesh again. Eddie B moaned.

Peg tugged the thread through. Linus watched her.

"I don't mean to hurt you," she said as though reading his thoughts.

She took fourteen stitches in his side. When she was done he was soaked with his own sweat.

She grinned at him and chirped, "All done," in the most cheerful way.

He didn't say thank you. She didn't expect it. He owed her some games. He owed her a piece of his time.

"Son of a bitch," Eddie B said in stunned admiration, emphasizing each syllable as though he were saying a prayer.

"Son of a bitch."

20.

Just as there's no Oriental Avenue station on any of New York's subways, there's no Boardwalk either. Or any street by that name.

There's no Boardwalk, but there is a Coney Island and that's got a boardwalk that runs along the Atlantic shore.

"Somewhere out in Coney Island?" Posner said.

Gertie and Limey and Mercado all nodded their heads. Malloy just sat there wishing all the killers who prowled his trains would take a rest. Would drop dead or go away.

"We'll get this sonofabitch if we got to put a cop on every goddamn car on every goddamn train on every goddamn line that goes to Coney," Gertie vowed.

"There's six of them goes to Stillwell Avenue," Malloy said.

"Don't you think I know that?" Gertie snapped.

"Just mentioning it. I won't tell you how many trains run those six lines. You probably already know."

"How many?" Gertie finally challenged.

"Too many," Malloy said.

"We can't cover every car," Posner said. "I haven't got enough men for that. What will your people give us, Malloy?"

"My boss says he'll give you everything he can spare."

"Good."

"But."

"I'm waiting."

"He says we've got other security problems all over the place."

"I get his point. I've got a piece of a city to police," Posner said.

"We got all of the city on this one," Gertie said.

"I mean I got to worry about killings in the gutters, in the streets, in the houses, and on the roofs all over Manhattan South," Posner said.

Malloy shrugged. There was nothing new in saying there wasn't enough law enforcement to go around.

"Let's pack security into Stillwell Avenue station," Limey said.

Everyone pretended to think about it, as though consensus would regularize the random.

"We'll pack the station with undercover," Posner decided. "We'll have more on the trains. First thing anybody does if he thinks a crime's going down is call up above. We'll have every rolling unit ready to block off the stations along the lines six stations back."

They all looked at it, talked about it. In the end they figured it was as good a piece of tactics as any they could devise. They knew they'd have to be awful goddamn lucky to make a score this way. But, after all, that was really what most police work was all about. Just plain luck.

So they rode the trains. And nothing happened. Nobody

86

got murdered. Nobody got shoved off in front of one, or gunned down, or stabbed, bludgeoned, or axed.

For a week.

"It is so quiet on those subways I could cry," Honker said to Marsha.

"You're not wishing somebody should get killed?" she said.

"Of course not."

"That would be awful to want somebody to die just so you could make an arrest."

"I'm ashamed," Honker said. "But here I am riding back and forth during rush hour and off, weekdays and weekends, and it's so quiet. You know not too many people go to Coney in the winter?"

"What's to go to the beach when it's twenty degrees?" Marsha asked reasonably. "Who can swim in such water? Who can lie on the sand?"

"Malloy goes to Coney," Honker said.

"Does he leave the trains?"

"Once. Once I saw him leave the trains."

"Did he leave the tunnels? Did he go upstairs and actually go outdoors?"

"That once, he did."

Marsha was very, very interested in the strange Irishman named Malloy. She was sorry she wasn't in school, so she could do a paper on him, a man who practically lived in the subways when he didn't really have to.

She leaned across the breakfast table.

"What did he do?"

"He walked along the boardwalk with his hands in the pockets of his overcoat."

"That's all?"

"He stopped for a hot dog and an orange drink."

"You'd make a good detective, Ira," Marsha said.

"Not with this nose."

"It's a beautiful nose."

"Maybe it is, but it is something people look at, and detectives shouldn't stand out so much from the crowd."

"You keep watching Malloy," she said. "Did he see you following him?"

"I'm certain that he didn't."

"See, your nose doesn't stand out so much," Marsha said triumphantly.

The snow fell on the city. It had drifted a little bit on the window pane of Irma's bedroom. They'd stayed in this Sunday night. She'd made Malloy a meatloaf. He ate more than half of it, and that pleased her in a different way from the times he admired her figure.

She shifted in Malloy's arms.

"What're you thinking?" she asked.

"That was good meatloaf."

"You're quick, Malloy. What were you really thinking?"

"You don't want to know. You'll only get mad."

"You weren't thinking about meatloaf, and you weren't thinking about what we just did. You get hungry, you eat, then you forget about it."

"Just an animal," Malloy smiled.

"Yeah."

"Simple-minded."

"I wouldn't say that. But I know what you think about."

"What?"

"Your job."

He turned his head to look at her.

"What the hell, Irma. You and my job. That's all I got."

She almost cashed in on the opening, but didn't. She wasn't even sure being married to him would be as good as what they had.

"Talk about your job," she said.

"The crazy's quiet."

"The Monopoly Killer?"

"That's the one."

"Seagrave don't let up on it in his column."

"It sells papers," Malloy said wryly.

"Well, that's okay, then," she said, matching his sarcasm.

"I'm waiting for that killer."

"What's he doing?"

"I don't know."

"The moon affects some of those crazies. It really does."

"Yeah, I know that."

"If not the moon, some cycle."

"You know what I found out?"

"What?"

"That old man. The last one killed?"

"Yeah?"

"The old man was a member of one of the Six Companies."

Irma looked vague. She didn't know what the Six Companies could be.

"The old Tongs," Malloy explained. "Wherever the Chinese are, there's the Six Companies."

"Like the Mafia?"

"Tougher than the Mafia, once upon a time."

"So what are you saying?"

"I'm wondering if that Chinese guy hurt his assailant. I'm wondering if he didn't just get in one lick or two before he took that knife in the gut."

"If he's hurt bad enough he'll be coming in for help sooner or later. Maybe he'll even be coming in to Bellevue Emergency."

21.

They'd been holding their breaths waiting for the first copy-cat killing, although they wouldn't even whisper about it among themselves.

By the time it came, property cards from Monopoly games were turning up all over town, in the subways, tucked into the pages of newspapers bought by straight citizens, and even the kids were running a brisk trade in them.

The victim had been choked to death in a subway rest-room. His windpipe had been crushed and a wad of toilet paper shoved down his throat to make sure he was dead. He was a vagrant. No known address.

The game card left on his body said Electric Company. "Capitalist Dog" was written on it with a red marking pen.

"The guy that done this is as crazy as the other one," Gertie said, "but he isn't the same kind of crazy."

90

Unless the Monopoly Killer was changing his way of doing things dramatically, everyone agreed that Gertie was right.

"Let's hope . . ." Posner started to say, then didn't say it.

Everyone knew that what he was going to say, what they all were thinking, was that they had all better pray that every bedbug in New York didn't decide to jump on this particular whirligig.

They knew that madness was an infectious disease. Cities were particularly susceptible to the spread of a number of viruses—homicide, sexual assault, and riot, among them. The cops often saw themselves less as officers upholding the law than as plague doctors desperately trying to prevent the spread of a virulent fever.

The first "confessor" looking for publicity or public trial, even death if that was the only way to satisfy the need to be somebody in a faceless world, turned himself in the same day.

Marvin Gatspahl was thirty years old with the look of a man twice that age about the eyes and mouth. He was as pale as a corpse, not simply fair, but bloodless. He had the nervous habit of widening his eyes when anyone addressed a question to him. It served to produce an intense dislike in anyone who was forced to have any extended association with him, but no one had ever cared to tell him so.

"Did you have any reasons for these killings, Mr. Gatspahl?" Limey asked in his soothing English voice.

"Oh, yes," Gatspahl chirped, widening his eyes as though terribly startled.

"Can you tell me the reasons?"

"Different reasons for different killings," Gatspahl said.

Limey nodded his head understandingly. Gertie sat in the corner of the interrogation room and glared at the self-accused suspect. Malloy sat in another, finding the only shadow in the place, his hands in his pockets as usual.

"Shall we start with the first one?" Limey purred.

"Morrison. That would be Morrison," Gatspahl said.

"That's right. Why did you stab Mr. Morrison?"

"He was a Jew."

"I see," Limey agreed softly. He liked the process, the slow questions building one on top of another in orderly progression. He flicked his eyes toward Gertie, begging his partner not to spoil the string by making some disgusted and impatient comment. Gertie nodded and sighed as though he'd heard his partner's request and was ready to indulge him.

"Mr. Gatspahl, aren't you a Jew?"

"I was a Jew. I'm no longer a Jew."

"You've converted to another faith?"

"No."

"You've just given up your own?"

"No."

"I don't understand."

"My Jewishness was burnt away."

"Ah."

"In the ovens."

"Which ovens would they be, Mr. Gatspahl?" Limey asked without change of expression or tone.

"Dachau. Bergen-Belsen. Chelmno. Auschwitz."

His voice was growing very thin, threatening to break. Malloy winced. He felt a little pain under his heart, the grip of sympathy.

"Mr. Gatspahl," Limey said very kindly, "you were not yet born when the world was at war."

Gatspahl laughed then. It rattled the one-way mirror set in the wall. It climbed the register until it became the piercing cry of a bat. It stopped abruptly when Gatspahl grasped his own throat in a clawlike hand.

"Now this second murder," Limey went on as though nothing odd had happened.

"Execution," Gatspahl said.

"Yes. The woman."

"Mrs. Spector. Also a Jew."

Malloy got up and left the room. The man was mad. The man could even be a killer, although he was more likely a victim looking for someone to kill him. Whatever he was, Malloy was certain he wasn't the one he was looking for.

It was nicely gloomy in the bar around the corner from Manhattan South. Malloy sometimes stopped in for a drink when the days got too long. He heard Seagrave before he could see him, felt the reporter's hand on his sleeve, pulling him onto the stool next to him, before he could see his face.

"What's your pleasure, Martin?" Seagrave asked.

"Rye and ginger," Malloy said.

"Set them up, Harry," Seagrave said to the bartender.

He started to push a bill across for the drink, but Malloy put his own two bucks on the bar and said, "I'll buy my own."

"You mad at me?"

"No."

"What then?"

"I've got something to tell you, and I don't like to drink a man's drink when I tell him he's a troublemaker."

"I've heard it before." Seagrave laughed sharply.

"Sure you have. Only this time I'm telling you, and that means something to me."

Seagrave turned a solemn face to Malloy.

"Let me have it."

"You should let the Monopoly Killings drop."

"It sells papers."

"Maybe. And maybe the good old days of circulation wars

and scoops and press cards stuck in hat bands are over. Television fixed it. What you're doing isn't reporting news, it's making up stories that cause trouble."

"What's happened?"

"The first genuine madman just walked into Manhattan South. He's up there puking out some old nightmares into Limey's ear. The cop's got to listen because maybe, just a little bit maybe, the gazoonie's the one who knifed those people, though it's very unlikely."

Seagrave shifted on the bar stool as though about to leave. Malloy put his hand on his arm.

"Don't. Wait until your inside informant gives you this. If you act on what I'm telling you this minute, I'll see you in the tunnels some night."

"Jesus Christ," Seagrave said in wonderment. "Are you coming on heavy with me?"

Malloy closed his eyes and removed his hand. He shook his head slowly.

"Hell, I'm no crusher, Seagrave. But you're not going to use me the way you're using everybody else or I'll break your arm or leg. So stay awhile."

Seagrave relaxed and quickly drank off his own highball. "Another," he said to the bartender.

When it came, Malloy shoved two bills across the wood to pay for it.

"On me," he said. "I've had my say. Think about it. People are getting hurt for no reason every day. Why rock the boat?"

Malloy walked out and Seagrave drank the glass empty. He wondered how he could work the moment into a story without bringing Malloy down on his back.

"The name of the game's 'save your own ass,' " he said. When Harry asked him what he'd said, Seagrave just shook his head.

22.

When Linus went looking for help he didn't go to Bellevue.
He was closest to Lenox Hill when the stitches busted open.
The stink of the infection made him sick to his stomach. It
scared him, too.

He had a fever. It was affecting his sense of time. He'd
lost a couple of days somewhere. He hadn't seen old Peg for
a while. He'd just stayed holed up in the Con Ed tunnel he'd
staked out long ago.

The city was covered with a thin blanket of snow that got
dirty almost on contact. The cops riding the lines to Coney
were bored, but warm.

Malloy rode the subways too. He was never bored down
there among the roar of the trains, and the pushing crowds,
and the wild winds that came sweeping through the tunnels.

Honker rode the trains like a minnow in the wake of a

whale. Wherever Malloy went, Honker went, a car or two away. He was getting to be a pretty good tail. Malloy never spotted him. At least, if he did he never acted as though he'd noticed.

Linus went to the emergency ward at Lenox Hill about ten o'clock Friday night. The gay attendant on duty could tell the good-looking young man was sick just by looking at his eyes.

"You come right on through here and sit down while I take down some information," he said, opening the half door into his crummy office.

He went through it all.

"Name?"

"Lima Bean," Linus said, his lips so numb he could hardly feel them touch.

"Oh, yes," the attendant said, but wrote it down the way he heard it. He understood about names.

"Address?"

"Vanderbilt Avenue," Linus said naming the site of the tunnel where he usually slept just beneath the Yale Club.

"That's a big street," the attendant lisped.

"Forty-fourth."

"If you say so."

The attendant asked Linus questions and Linus lied. It didn't really much matter. The attendant just needed the paper. He took Linus into the treatment area. Every cubicle was full.

"Shit," the attendant said. "Come right over here. Hop right up here."

He patted a gurney with a dirty sheet stretched on it as though it were a marriage bed. Linus struggled to get on it, but couldn't make it. The attendant helped him and grabbed a little feel.

"Don't mess around with me," Linus said evenly.

The attendant backed off in a huff and left Linus sitting there.

96

After a while Linus began to moan to himself. He rocked back and forth like a child comforting itself.

An intern finally came over to see what was the matter.

"You got a number?" he asked, pulling at Linus's jacket lapels. Linus slapped his hand away angrily.

"What number?" he demanded.

"Treatment room number."

"Nobody gave me anything," Linus mumbled. "Don't hurt me."

"Hey, Kenny," the doctor called. The attendant came out of his office and sauntered over.

"This guy's got no number," the doctor said.

"I give him a number. Maybe he lost his number," the attendant lied. "You lose your number, fella?"

Linus stared at the man through his fevered eyes.

"Don't mess around with me," he warned again.

"Go into that cubicle mister, and watch your mouth. We don't need this kind of shit. Right there. Right there," the doctor urged as Linus allowed himself to be half helped, half pushed off the gurney toward one of the examination booths.

"That's right. We don't need it," the attendant echoed, then started to go back to his window.

"Where the hell you going?" the doctor asked. "Stay with it. I might be needing you."

They got Linus up on another gurney in the examination cubicle. Linus watched them like an animal at bay as they helped him take off his shirt to expose the clumsily bandaged wound.

The doctor removed the pad of rags.

"Jesus Christ, what butcher sewed you up?"

"Fix it," Linus said.

"Where'd you get a cut like that?" the doctor asked.

"Looks like a stab wound to me," the attendant remarked.

Linus backed off and put his hands up as though ready to fight.

"Watch what you say, dammit," the doctor whispered fiercely. "This sucker might be delirious."

"Got it in the subway," Linus said. "Somebody cut me in the subway."

"Christ, maybe the Monopoly Killer took a shot at him."

"The people in the subway laugh at me," Linus mumbled.

"He could be hallucinating," the doctor said in a low aside. "Lay back down there, Mr. —" He turned his head to the attendant. "What's his name? What's his name?" he whispered.

"Bean. His name's Lima Bean."

"Is that what he said?"

"I wouldn't make that up, would I?"

"He's definitely hallucinating. Nurse! Goddammit, nurse!" the doctor yelled. Even before she hit the doorway he was calling for a syringe of Novocaine, and a surgical kit for the debridement of the wound. As she turned in the doorway to go fetch, he thought about an IV of saline in case of shock, an ampule of Demerol to calm Linus down, and a course of antibiotics for the infection.

Linus took the needle pricks necessary to deaden the area around the wound, watching the procedure as he leaned back on his elbows, as if he doubted the doctor's intentions. He watched as the doctor took the scalpel and cut away the morbid tissue and cause the wound to bleed freely once again. By this time he seemed to have come to the conclusion that the doctor didn't mean to kill him.

As the intern started to stitch him up again, Linus mumbled something.

"What'd he say?" the doctor asked.

"Said 'Mumblety Peg can sew pretty good too,'" the attendant answered.

"Wonder she didn't kill him," the doctor said.

The nurse, setting the IV needle into the back of Linus's hand, agreed.

98

"Definitely a screwball," the doctor nodded wisely.

The nurse injected the Demerol into the IV feed. Then she slipped in the needle for the antibiotic drip. Linus was staring at her. She left the room the first chance she got. There was something about the staring boy she didn't like.

The doctor cleaned up, dressed the wound, taped a bandage tight over it.

"Find him a bed for the night," he told the attendant.

"You're joking," the attendant muttered under his breath, but the doctor was already out of the room. "Calling Dr. Kildare," the attendant said a little louder.

He turned to get Linus back into his shirt. He put his hands on Linus's arm and Linus sat straight up. He swung a hard fist at the attendant's nose and started screaming all the filthy obscenities a life in the gutter and the tunnels had taught him. The doctor was back in the cubicle, shouting for a nurse and all the orderlies he could get.

There was half a dozen on him by the time Linus was subdued momentarily.

"Where you want him?" an orderly panted.

"Out of here," the doctor said. "I'm calling Bellevue. This asshole's psycho. Somebody call for a city ambulance."

They tagged him, stuck his admitting papers in an envelope, which they gave to the driver of the ambulance, and shipped Linus out. The intern got on the phone and called Bellevue. The psychiatrist there agreed to accept the patient and Lenox Hill emergency settled down.

At Bellevue psychiatric emergency, the admitting physician took one look at Linus's condition and ordered him taken to medical emergency for clearance.

Linus landed in Irma Sweet's ward forty-five minutes later. The weekend slaughter was just starting to pour in. Knifings. Auto accidents. Wife and husband beatings. Rapes, muggings, and assorted assaults.

Linus had quieted down. It was easier to let him walk in.

The resident, dead on his feet, gave the orderly the thumb. Gerry Godowski hauled Linus over to a chair and sat him down.

A siren called out two blocks away. A second eerie voice joined in. Two cops came slamming in through the doors.

"Five-car wreck on Roosevelt Drive," one of them said.

Godowski looked at the sheet on Linus.

"That your name?" he asked. "Is Lima Bean really your name?"

"I want to tell you—" Linus started to say, then forgot what it was. "I'm really tired," he said.

Ambulances came braking up to the entrance, sirens dying like the screams of slaughtered men.

"Godowski!" Irma Sweet yelled. The orderly turned away.

"I want to tell you," Linus said to no one, "what I been doing down in the tunnels. I'm the one's been killing those people who come crawling around down there where I live."

The smashed-up people came stumbling in or carried in on stretchers. Linus went over to Irma directing traffic in her bloody butcher's apron.

"I want to tell you what I done," he said.

Irma looked him over in a second. She saw the bulge of the bandage under his shirt, and the look of stunned confusion in his eyes.

Malloy came up beside her. She turned to look at him.

"Just stopping by. I can see this isn't the time," he said.

"No, love," she said. He kissed her quickly and walked away.

"Malloy," she called.

When he turned around she said, "You can't hunt that subway killer day and night. We can only do what we can do."

He nodded and smiled and left the place. Irma turned back to Linus. She looked at him carefully again and decided he could wait.

100

"Sit down over there," she said. She hurried over to a young girl lying on a stretcher whose face had been half chopped away.

Linus looked at the door where Malloy had gone out into the street. He'd seen the Transit cop plenty of times before. He'd ducked him often enough while he was playing the student dodge. Now he knew Malloy was hunting him.

The girl on the stretcher screamed.

Linus walked out of Emergency. He went along the corridor to a door that led to the stairwell. He walked down several flights of steps that led down into one sub-basement after another. At the deepest one he walked along the wall to a door painted green. It opened into a Con Edison tunnel.

He ran through it to Lexington, staggering along, afraid that he would fall down and die. At 28th he slipped through another door something like the first. He was at the end of the 28th Street station. He walked the length of it. At the other end he jumped down onto the tracks and walked into the darkness of the tunnel mouth.

Two cleaning women, on their way to work, looked at each other and shrugged. What was there to say about the screwballs in the city?

23.

March came in like a lion. The rain poured down and washed the dirty old snow down the sewers and revealed the dirty old streets underneath.

It was Sunday night again. In several hours Malloy would go and pick up Irma. Next week her shift would change. She'd work graveyard for six weeks. He'd rearrange his hours, too, so they'd have Monday morning breakfast together. Irma said his shift didn't count for anything, since he was nearly always down in the tunnels anyhow.

He lay on his back on the couch that made up into a bed when he took the bother. A can of beer sat on the table nearby, going flat. The black and white television flickered in the gloom. The volume was turned down very low.

Once he'd had an apartment in Brooklyn Heights. Now

he lived in a residence hotel near Union Square. Once he'd had a wife. Now he lived alone with a television set. She'd loved television. He couldn't relate to it. He knew what life was really like. He had four bullet scars to prove it. Their last argument started over getting a color set. It seemed as good a reason as any to end a failed marriage. She bought a twenty-seven-inch monster with part of her settlement.

He didn't feel unhappy. He didn't think of happiness as something you could hold on to and look at. He was comfortable when he was with Irma, and there was something joyous in it when he made love to her. Even after two years. He was happy when he was in the tunnels.

He had the odd disease every cop suffers from. On the one hand he was weary and sick of the things that people did, and of the people themselves for that matter, yet he never felt really good unless he was right in among them, rubbing asses, rubbing bellies.

He got up off the couch and grabbed his coat. Lightning shattered the night outside the window. He grabbed his crushed tweed hat and jammed it on his head. He slammed the door and hurried into the rain.

He went down the stairs into the BMT station in Union Square. There was a place to eat underground where you could get a quarter of a flat loaf, sliced and oiled, filled with green peppers, sausage, and onion.

"Whattaya know, Larry?" Malloy greeted the kid behind the counter.

"Fachrissake, Malloy, how many times I gotta tell you my name's Tony?"

"How long you work here?"

"Nine months."

"Larry worked here twelve years. When you work here twelve years I'll call you Tony," Malloy teased.

"You want an orange with that?"

Malloy nodded, and the kid scooped up some crushed

ice and poured in an orange-colored drink that tasted vaguely of chemical.

"What do you see?" Malloy asked.

"The usual."

"Anybody fit that description I gave you?"

"If I had a penny."

Malloy knew what he meant. There were hundreds of young guys wearing nothing more than sweaters and scarves traveling the subway. Some didn't have far to go through the weather from home to job. Some liked to tough it out.

"You'll keep looking?"

"What else I got to do?" Tony said, and waved to Malloy as the Transit cop took his sandwich and caught the 4 going out to Crown Heights.

The car was half full. It wasn't a working crowd. There were some, of course. In a city nowadays there are people working every day, seven days a week. There were some types slick as cream, shirts unbuttoned to the second rib, pants tight around their asses. They were on their way to some disco or some dance out in Brooklyn. Small town girls out in Brooklyn.

Malloy left the 4 at Fulton Street. He walked up and down the platform. Moving. Moving. That's what it was about riding the trains. Always moving. He took the free transfer to the A Train, Rockaway Shuttle, and got out at the next stop, Jay Street Borough Hall.

Linus boarded the number 6 at Grand Central Station ten minutes after Malloy stepped into the 4 Lexington, and found himself a seat along the side. He wondered how many of the people, dressed in their Sunday best, were coming home from Grandma's house over in Queens or the Bronx. The husbands looked oddly uncomfortable in their suits and ties. The wives looked determined that the family should be together, and decently dressed, at least one day of the week.

104

A little girl in a pink dress and Mary Janes flirted with Linus. He winked and she hid her face in her mother's side.

Eddie B, pushing the antique wooden, cane-bottomed wheelchair, got on at Bleecker Street. He sat next to Linus.

"Where you going?" he asked.

"Riding," Linus said. "Where you going, Eddie B?"

"Riding."

They jostled each other gently, moving with the sway of the car.

At Spring Street Eddie B spoke again.

"How far?"

"Brooklyn Bridge," Linus said after a pause. "You?"

"Anywhere. Maybe catch the J out to East River Park. Unless you'd like some company?"

Linus pretended to think about it. Finally he shook his head.

Eddie B kept looking at Linus with bright, squirrel-like eyes. He was looking for a friend.

At Canal, Eddie didn't move to get off.

"You can transfer over to J from here," Linus informed him.

Eddie B shrugged.

"I can catch it from Brooklyn Bridge. Transfer up to Chambers."

Linus nodded affably, but the coin of pain began to throb between his eyes.

When the train pulled into its last stop, Brooklyn Bridge, everybody got off. Eddie B walked alongside Linus, shoulder to shoulder, pushing the old wheelchair along. One of the wheels screeched. They bumped into each other gently.

Linus stepped away elaborately.

"What's the matter, the tunnel isn't wide enough for you?"

"Sorry," Eddie B mumbled, and looked sidelong at Linus, wondering what was eating the kid.

105

"What's eating you, kid?" he asked, the thought being mother to the deed.

Linus kept on walking upstairs and down until they came to the platform where the M stopped on the way to Coney. Eddie B stood alongside him, hands in pocket, lips pursed as he whistled a soundless tune.

"I thought you were going to East River Park," Linus asked. There was an edge to his voice, but Eddie B didn't seem to hear it.

"Maybe I go out to Prospect Park instead. That's a nice park."

"What the hell you going to a park for after dark anyhow?" Eddie B leered at Linus.

"I ask you a question and you grin at me like a goddamn idiot?" Linus exploded.

Eddie B took three steps back toward the edge of the platform. Linus advanced on him.

"Couples go to the parks at night. They go at it underneath the bushes," Eddie B said quickly.

"Maybe in summer they do that. Maybe then. It's raining cats and dogs up there. Nobody's going to be out in the rain, underneath a bush, doing any goddamn thing."

Eddie B backed off another step.

The M train came roaring into the station. Linus raised his hands. Eddie B got behind his chair.

Malloy got on the F train going to Coney Island. If there's anything bleaker than Coney in the winter or early spring, it's Coney in the rain. If there's anything gloomier than Coney in the rain, it's Coney in the rain at nine o'clock and after. Malloy stared at his feet. He looked at the cracks between the skinny grid of the floor. He thought he saw a seashell, but it was only a half-sucked mint somebody had spit out.

The closer he got to Stillwell Avenue, end of the line, the emptier the car became. Not many were going to Coney on

a wet Sunday night in March. Most everybody who wanted
to be in Coney was already there.

Linus and Eddie B sat on the M train. Neither one had
said a word since they'd boarded, and now the train was
in the tunnel under the East River on the way to Brooklyn.

"I thought you was going to push me in front of the train,"
Eddie B said. His words were oddly conversational, but
there was a thin line of strain and old fear running through
them.

"Why would I want to do that, Eddie B?" Linus asked
evenly, his eyes holding on to the derelict's with an intensity
that would have unnerved anyone more aware than Eddie B.

"I don't know." He thought about it. Then he laughed
nervously. "Maybe because I was getting on your nerves."

"That what you think, Eddie B?"

"Well. Maybe?"

"Well, maybe you were right. But, you see, I don't think
I'd want to snuff anybody I knew."

"That's right, you know me."

"I do. I know you well enough to be able to say you're
going to be getting off first stop in Brooklyn."

"Court Street."

"That's right. You'll be getting off, won't you?"

Eddie B was about to dispute that, but then he suddenly
and finally got the message in Linus's eyes.

"Hey, I got you," he said. "You don't want no company."

"You're very smart, Eddie B," Linus said.

The train pulled in and Eddie B got off, leaving Linus
alone except for a girl dressed in a spring dress, too thin for
the weather, with a heavy sweater over it. She had a trans-
parent plastic slicker on top of everything and a plastic hood
over her hair. It was tied under her chin with pink cords.
She was reading a paperback book.

Linus didn't have Eddie B to stare at any more so he
stared at the girl. She fidgeted a little, then deliberately

107

caught herself and settled down very still. She didn't want the man to know she was aware of him. That was bad subway defense tactics.

They stopped at Lawrence Street. She looked out at the signs on the platform as though she were coming near the end of her ride, only a stop or two away. It was a sign that "nobody" should bother wasting time trying to pick her up since she wouldn't be riding long enough for it to do "somebody" any good.

At DeKalb a half a dozen people got on. She sighed and visibly relaxed. Linus studied the graffiti that was everywhere. His mark was up there on some of the cars.

Malloy got off the F train at West 8th, where the New York Aquarium was. He crossed over to the 6th Avenue Express platform going back to the Bronx. He didn't seem to be doing much of anything. He wasn't doing much of anything except looking for any young kid in a sweater, and maybe a scarf, acting as though he was heading nowhere, just like Malloy.

It was half past nine. Maybe a little later. He was sorry he'd left the room. He felt wet even though he'd been underground long enough to dry out, more or less. His coat and hat smelled like the coat of a mangy dog. The D train came in. He sat down gratefully.

Linus stepped out after the girl just before the doors closed at Prospect Park station. He followed her casually, making it a point not to be seen looking at her when she glanced back at him. Her heels made little tapping sounds that tapped right back from the tiled walls. They weren't far from the Brooklyn Museum. Maybe there was something going on there. A concert or something. He could go there and sit with the other people listening to the chamber music or whatever. But he knew that they would know he was a tunnel-dweller. They'd whisper behind his back. He'd

108

catch them looking at him just a split second after they stopped looking at him.

The girl was taking the underpass to Prospect Park station. There were four stops on the Franklin Avenue Shuttle. Botanic Gardens, Franklin Avenue, Park Place, and—

"What?" he said as though someone had spoken to him.

Park Place. Something had happened of importance at Park Place.

"Not the one in Brooklyn," he said aloud.

The girl looked at him and started walking much faster.

Linus turned around and went back. He got on the D train going to Coney.

Plenty of riders for some reason. They got off at Church and Newkirk and nobody got on.

There were only two of them left on the car. He was at one end and the girl was at the other. At first he thought it was the same girl. Print skirt clinging to her legs, heavy sweater over it, making what was supposed to look dainty clumsy. Over that a plastic raincoat and a hood. She was reading a book. She even looked a little like the other girl, except her rain hood was tied on with blue tapes.

Linus got up and started walking down the length of the car. He felt better. Even the pain between his eyes seemed to be going away. He was grinning. He intended to tell this girl just how funny life was. How, just a minute before, he'd been sitting across from a girl dressed exactly like her. Only on the M train.

The girl looked up at Linus as he approached. She closed her book in her lap and then stared at the cover as though she were still deeply absorbed in the reading of it.

"Know what?" Linus said.

"Get away from me. Please, get away from me," she said. She knew from the look in his eye that this was no ordinary subway masher. This was danger, or injury. It could even be death.

"Hey, I want to tell you something funny," Linus said.

The girl looked around wildly. They were alone. The express whipped through Avenue M. The next express stop where she could get off and run was King's Highway.

Malloy caught himself nodding off. He looked out of the window. They were just pulling out of the station at Avenue U. Next stop King's Highway. He put his hat down over his eyes. He figured he'd go home and sleep for an hour before going to pick up Irma. Maybe they'd have Greek tonight even if he wasn't very hungry.

The girl tried to stand up when Linus sat next to her.
"Don't do that," he said, grabbing her wrist.
She jerked away and opened her mouth to scream. The train's brakes screeched as it pulled into King's Highway. For a moment both the girl and Linus thought the sound had come from her. Linus stood up and grabbed for her. He caught the skirt of her raincoat as she started to run. He pulled back and she was jerked off her feet.

Malloy's train pulled into King's Highway. He raised his hat to make sure he knew where he was. Across the platform the train to Coney was stopped. A man was bending over something on the floor. His arm flashed up and down. Something glittered in his hand. The second time it rose there was a splash of red.

Malloy was on his feet and yelling as the doors closed on the other train and it started pulling out. The doors to his own car closed in his face. He hammered on them as the train lurched into motion. He pulled the emergency, but the train to Coney bearing the killer and his victim was already speeding into the tunnel.

He looked around. There wasn't a uniform in sight. A few people were sticking themselves partway out of the doors of the train he'd been on, wondering what the hell was going

110

on. Then he saw Honker running toward him from down the line.

"He's done it again," he yelled out to Honker, then turned on his heel and started running down the platform as though imagining he could catch the express on foot.

He stopped at the tunnel mouth, turned, and ran just as fast back to where Honker was sending out the call for mobile units to cordon off the stations at Sheepshead Bay and Brighton Beach.

"Arrest everybody on the Coney Island Express," Honker shouted. "We got the killer bottled up."

24.

There were cops everywhere on the streets. Not only around the Sheepshead Bay and Brighton Beach stations, but at Avenue U and Neck Road, the local stops between, as well.

The D train never got to Brighton. It was caught at Sheepshead and held up at the platform there.

There were uniforms and plain clothes sweeping through the station from one end to the other, combing the train as they went along, herding everyone aboard before them like so many sheep. The only one they didn't pick up in the dragnet was the girl in the plastic raincoat who was lying on her back, blood all over her chest and hands.

Up above, police cars came speeding in from every direction. They skidded to stops that dried the streets under the tires for a second. There was more than one collision. They filled the mouths of every exit. A mouse couldn't get out.

Honker and Malloy arrived in a police car. They went down into the station and saw thirty or forty people crowded together in one spot, watching the cops who were surrounding them as though they were going to kill them.

Posner saw Malloy and beckoned him over. Gertie and Limey were nearby telling everybody to shut up, that things were all right.

Things weren't all right. Nothing was all right and it soon became obvious that the killer wasn't bottled up.

"Where'd he go? Where'd he go?" Gertie complained.

He looked at Malloy as though he had the answer.

"How come you got so many goddamn little doors down in these tunnels?" Gertie said.

"I didn't build them," Malloy said.

Posner came up.

"You put in the call, Malloy?"

Malloy shook his his head and nodded toward Honker.

"Your man did."

"You see the crime go down?" Posner asked Sergeant Levine.

"No, sir."

"How come you put in the call?"

"I was on the uptown train."

"Who saw it go down?"

"Malloy."

"Okay, back to you, Malloy. What did you see?"

"The trains were both stopped at King's Highway. They were both practically empty. The car across the platform looked empty too, at first. Then I saw this arm with something flashing in it raise up, and I saw this guy bending over something. Somebody. The second time his arm raised up I knew he had a knife in his hand because there was blood on it and him."

"Can you give us a description?"

"Not a hell of a lot more than we got from Charlie Spiers, and Mrs. Gottlieb and the other Hadassah ladies. I just had

113

the three-quarter view of him from the back. Seemed young just like they said. Brown hair. He was wearing a blue sweater and a scarf."

"Good work," Gertie said. "Now we got only half a million nut cases to sort out."

"What color was the scarf?" Posner asked, ignoring Gertie.

"Striped. Blue, black, and white, I think."

Posner turned to Gertie. "Put that out on the radio. Maybe we'll get lucky."

He looked expectantly at Malloy for a minute while Malloy thought about what he'd seen. Finally he shook his head and shrugged.

"You got everything I got."

The cops and detectives walked away except for Honker.

"Thanks for trying to throw me a piece of the credit."

"What the hell, you were out riding the lines when practically nobody else was. Your own time?"

Honker nodded.

"You were riding the lines, too."

"Well, it's sort of like my own backyard, you know?"

The train had been shunted off, the car with the body in it disconnected as before. Now the passengers were all back in it, going on home or wherever. Honker and Malloy watched it go into the tunnel.

"How the hell did that shithead get past everybody?" Honker mused.

"Off the end of the train," Malloy said. "How dumb can I get? He waited for the train to slow down as it came into the station, opened the back door, and jumped onto the track. Nobody would be able to see him."

Malloy started to run.

"Where you going?" Honker panted, running alongside.

"All the way to Coney."

They ran together down staircases and tunnels and underpasses. They ran up others. They got to the platform

114

just as the M train downtown was closing its doors. Malloy grabbed hold. The conductor told him to let go, then saw who it was and activated the mechanism again. The doors hissed open and Malloy was aboard with Honker right behind him.

"We try Brighton, then we try West 8th before we get to the end of the line," Malloy said.

There were a few people on the Brighton station platform, but nobody who fit the description. There was a man selling papers at the foot of the stairs. Malloy asked him if he'd seen a young kid, wearing a sweater and a striped scarf.

"No, I didn't. You want a paper?"

Malloy shook his head. He ran back to the train. Honker was talking to the conductor, holding the train until Malloy had his chance to look around.

Malloy got on board.

"Christ, it's only a long shot. No reason for him to lolly-gag around at a time like this," Malloy said, more to himself than to anyone.

At the Aquarium station Malloy got off again. He was about to get back on when he saw a young man wearing a sweater and a scarf starting up the stairs. The sweater was blue. The kid glanced back and saw Malloy hurrying after him.

"Hold it," Malloy yelled.

The kid took off up the stairs as though his tail was burned.

Honker left the train on the run.

"Go on. Go on," he shouted to the conductor.

The conductor stayed where he was between the cars, one hand on the door lever. He watched as Malloy pounded up the stairs after the runaway.

Honker started after them, then thought better of it and ran back to the other entrance on the south side.

Malloy raced after the kid. The rain was coming down harder. It struck the street and blurred the pavement. The running man splashed through the puddles without trying to avoid them, haring straight ahead with all possible speed. He ducked down the mouth of the station across the street. Malloy was right after him.

When the kid burst onto the platform again he almost collided head-on into Honker. The policeman jerked himself out of the way, lost his footing, and went sprawling on the cement. He got up shaking his hand. It hurt like hell where it'd been scraped in the fall. The runner was undecided about which way to go. The doors of the train were still open. The runner went inside and ran along the length of a car, jerking at each door and slamming it shut behind him.

Malloy ran into the train. Honker was already there.

"Close the doors," Honker was yelling. "Close the goddamn doors."

The conductor was slow. When he hit the valve release the runner was already through two cars away and on the platform again. Honker almost got trapped, but managed to grab the doors before they could close again. They slammed open. Honker was out and so was Malloy.

They raced after the kid, who started up the stairway again, but tripped and sprawled out on the bottom steps. By the time he was on his feet again, Malloy and Honker had him.

Honker slammed him up against the wall. At their backs the conductor finally remembered his schedule. The doors closed and the train pulled out.

Malloy picked up the scarf that had fallen from the young man's shoulders. It was dark green with a red stripe in it. Honker was patting the kid down. The runner was panting. He looked over his shoulder wide-eyed, scared half out of his wits.

"I got no money. I got no money," he kept protesting. "For Christ's sake don't hit me. I'm sorry I got no money."

"I don't want your goddamn money," Honker rasped.

116

"Where's the knife?"

"What the hell you talking about?"

"Let him go, Honker," Malloy said.

"What?"

"Let him go. He's not the one."

He held out the scarf.

"You can turn around," he said to the stranger. The kid turned around with his arms ready to protect his face in case they were setting him up for a beating.

"It's all right," Malloy soothed. "Just a mistake."

"A mistake?" the kid said tentatively.

"That's right. Just a mistake. We thought you were somebody else."

The kid grabbed the scarf out of Malloy's hand. Now that danger was past he was indignant.

"Who the hell you think I was?"

"I guess we owe you that much," Malloy said. "We thought you were the Monopoly Killer."

The kid smiled vaguely. It was nice to be mistaken for a celebrity.

25.

The near miss had Malloy unsettled. Well, it really hadn't been a near miss. Shaking the hell out of a kid spooked by scare headlines was nothing like a near miss. Still and all, the frustration of it was enough to set Malloy on edge.

He called Irma at Bellevue and told her what had happened and how he felt.

"I won't be good company," he said.

"You'll be better company than none at all. And I'll be better company for you than an empty room," she replied.

He didn't answer her.

When the silence stretched on too long Irma spoke up again.

"You don't have to pick me up at the hospital. I'll get home alone. But I'll expect you at my place. You hear me, Malloy?"

"Yeah. When?"

"When you get there. I'm not putting a clock on you. When you get there."

"All right."

"I'll fix us something to eat at home," Irma said.

"How about I bring Chinese?" Malloy asked.

"Good idea," Irma said cheerily, "but tell them no goddamn MSG."

Malloy hung up the phone. He sat in the booth and read the filthy graffiti scrawled on the walls and windows, nearly as thick as it was on the train cars. Everybody wanted to be somebody.

He shivered and came out of the daze he'd fallen into. He rode the trains over to Grand Central. He looked at the magazine racks there, thumbing through the girly magazines, wondering why such beautiful women would want to spread their legs and show everything. Did they think displaying themselves that way would attract the attention of a motion picture or television producer? Was it just the considerable pay they got for posing? Did it really matter any more?

"Ho, Malloy," Barboo Maggione said. He jiggled the coins filling the pockets of his apron. "Some of that, huh, Malloy? What you couldn't do with some of that."

"You'd like it, huh, Barboo?" Malloy smiled.

Barboo made a face and vibrated his lips as though the very idea of such good fortune had just driven him mad.

"What's around?" Malloy asked.

"The usual. I don't get many hard types looking the mags over. Just a lot of wishers."

He went over to the rack of tabloids and jerked one out.

"You see this?"

There was a doctored photo on the front page of a faceless man holding a bloody knife in his fist. The blood was red and so was the headline about "The Monopoly Killer." Malloy looked for the byline. Seagrave was picking up extra

119

bucks. He thumbed through to page three. That header demanded to know why the New York Police Department couldn't do anything to find a madman who seemed free to strike anywhere at any time.

"Same old shit," Barboo said.

Malloy put the paper back and went back to the trains.

He dozed off on the 6 train going downtown to Greenwich Village. He had a dream. Not the nightmare of tunnels and dimly perceived gunmen, but a short dream in which time turned back. In it he was aware that he was a young man with a future, riding home to a wife as attractive as any in the centerfold of a girly magazine.

The train braking into a station woke him up with a start. The dream was still fresh, and for a moment he didn't know where the hell he was. He had an erection. He looked around guiltily and then realized his overcoat covered it.

He hurried off the train at Astor Place in the East Village. All of a sudden he wanted to be with Irma more than he'd ever wanted to be with a woman in his life.

He forgot all about stopping for Chinese.

Irma didn't care.

26.

The card found on Mary Finney's body was not a Monopoly property card. It was a Chance card.

The representative from Parker Brothers Games fingered the orange piece of pasteboard. He flicked the edge with a thumbnail.

"You see the question mark printed on the back?"

Posner nodded his head.

"That means it's from a deluxe set. We only print the backs on a deluxe set."

Gertie looked at Limey in disgust. They were really scraping bottom and everybody knew it. Everybody except the man from Parker Brothers. He thought he was telling them something useful. He believed the cops could describe a man's height, weight, and what he had for breakfast from a drop of sweat.

"Game's probably three years old. We don't use this grade of card stock any more. Not even for the deluxe game."

He said the word "deluxe" as though it had some magic to it.

Mercado picked his nose and Malloy leaned forward in his chair, peering out of the shadows in the corner of the office.

"That's all you can tell us?" Posner asked mildly.

"That's all," the man said, more than a little disappointed at the lack of reaction he was getting.

"Thank you very much. Will you leave your identification tag with the officer at the reception desk?" Posner said, standing up and extending his hand for a brief handshake.

"Was I any help to you?"

"I'd say so," Gertie drawled. "Wouldn't you say so, Officer Whittlesey?"

"Indeed-e-do," Limey said.

"You can tell your friends and relatives that you were a great help to the cops," Gertie said, with an edge to his voice.

The man left the office wondering just how in hell he'd offended the goddamn cops he was trying to help.

"No need for that," Posner said mildly. He didn't go any further than that. He knew Gertie's nerves were strung out tight. Just the day before he'd had to intervene in order to prevent the detective from taking a swing at the reporter, Seagrave.

Gertie made a noise of self-disgust and waved his hand in the air.

Malloy picked the little card off the desk. He looked at it for the hundredth time, hoping to find some answer on it.

"Whattaya see?" Gertie mocked him.

"A little character with his pockets turned inside out."

"And what does it say?"

122

" 'Pay poor tax of fifteen dollars.' "

Malloy put the card back on the desk. He sighed and looked out of the window as though he were uncomfortable being out and above ground.

"So whattaya know?" Gertie said.

"We're losing him."

"What the hell you talking about?" Gertie nearly shouted. "We never goddamn well had him."

"He was trying to talk to us at least. He was trying to talk to somebody."

Before Gertie could hoot at that Mercado spoke up softly.

"That's right. And he may still be trying to talk to us."

"Tell us all about it," Gertie said, sprawling back in his chair, challenging Mercado to do his dog and pony act. "Figure out what's going on in this asshole's head. Go ahead and dazzle us."

"Ah, ah, ah," Limey soothed.

Mercado grinned understandingly.

"One thing we know. You can never tell what a crazy man will do next."

"What's this we're eating?" Malloy asked Irma.

"Korean," she said.

"How long we been doing this?"

"Doing what?"

"Eating different nationalities every Sunday night?"

"Since last Easter."

"We ever eat the same twice?"

"Only when I make you meatloaf at home."

Malloy picked at his food.

"You don't like this Korean very much?" Irma asked.

"It's all right."

"No, you don't like it very much," she insisted, as though she'd invented it, cooked it, and was forcing it down his throat.

123

"It tastes fishy."

"It's seafood," Irma said flatly.

"It's all right."

"It was a crazy goddamn idea seeing how many times we could eat from a different country."

"Maybe we could write a book," Malloy smiled, trying to make it up.

He wondered if this was how big quarrels, the beginnings of endings, started. Like about television sets.

They ate in silence for a while.

"You feel it?" Irma finally said.

"I think so," Malloy said.

"It's in the air. Everybody's terrified, but they're afraid to say so. I listen to people talking about whether it's better to go home with the crowds or when the cars are a little emptier."

"It's worse down there in the tunnels," Malloy said. "People are looking at each other."

Irma looked at him in open surprise.

"You hear what you just said?"

"What?"

"You said that people are looking at each other."

"That's right."

"Well, isn't that a good thing? I mean shouldn't people look at each other?" Irma insisted.

Malloy thought about it. Thought about the way we take for granted that certain behavior is good behavior. How there's good behavior and bad behavior. There's only getting by. Survival.

"No, they shouldn't," Malloy said softly. "Not in any place as big and crowded as this city. Not in any place that's filled with strangers. I don't expect the average person will ever make a friend of someone they look at eye to eye across a subway aisle. Better to look at your newspaper. Better to look at the graffiti on the walls. I mean if strangers look at me all the time I've got no space left around me. Nowhere to be alone with my thoughts while I go from one place where I got problems to another place where I got problems."

"You make it sound like a ride on a subway is a vacation."

"Maybe," Malloy said. "Maybe."

He took a large forkful of food. He chewed it with apparent relish.

"This Korean food is good," he said.

"You are some crazy Irishman," Irma said.

27.

"What's in this stew?" Linus grumbled.

"You don't like it, you don't have to eat it," Peg said.

"I just asked you what it was."

"Cat," old Peg said flatly.

Linus looked feverish around the eyes, but he wasn't really sick any more. He looked at her intensely. He wondered if she meant it. He suspected she put cat in her stews sometimes. And sometimes rat.

"It's good," Linus said.

"You ought to go back to the hospital. You still look feverish to me," Peg said.

"They wouldn't help me. I tried to tell the nurse. She told me to sit down and wait."

"So?"

"Said she'd be with me in a minute. She wouldn't have been back to help me in a minute."

Peg nodded her head sagely, like one who was very much experienced in such humiliations.

"They always used to tell me to sit down and wait a minute when I went to get food stamps," she said.

Linus frowned as if he were annoyed that she was trying to take a free ride on his anger.

"They used to tell me to sit down and wait in the clinic too."

"Yeah?"

"And at the welfare office."

"Yeah?"

"I told them what they could do with their food stamps, and their medicine, and their welfare."

"I feel all right," Linus said. They were holding separate conversations.

"You still look sick to me. You finished?"

Linus stared into the styrofoam cup from which he was spooning the stew.

"I guess," he said and threw it on the floor.

Peg picked it up and put it into a paper bag with some other trash. She clucked her tongue, abusing him and his careless habits.

When she was done she started laying out a backgammon board.

"No Monopoly?" Linus said slyly.

Peg looked up to see him grinning at her triumphantly.

"Somebody stole nearly all of it," she said. "Not just some more of the properties. Somebody stole the Chance cards. All of them."

"That's lousy," Linus said. "That's a lousy thing to do."

"Yeah, yeah, yeah," old Peg moaned.

"A really lousy thing to do." Linus started to giggle. The pain between his eyes seemed to be whirling about like a pinwheel.

"Whoever done it ought to be shot," Peg yelled.

"Strung up by his thumbs," Linus laughed.

"Ought to be shot and cut up in pieces," Peg raved on. Little patches of foam were gathering at the corners of her mouth. That seemed to be very funny as far as Linus was concerned. He started to shriek uncontrollably.

"Goddamn. Goddamn," Peg fumed.

"Oh, I say goddamned and Amen, too," Linus raged on.

"Why'd you do it? Why'd you goddamn steal the pieces of my game, you cruel young son of a bitch?" Peg screamed at the top of her lungs.

Her words rattled down the steam pipe, resounding off the walls like the scattering of BB shot. They filled the space with a rage and horror that could not be contained in the words alone.

Silence fell. It had a weight and presence all its own.

"I never had a Monopoly set when I was a kid. I never had any game at all," he said very softly. He stared at her as though she were to blame for that and all the childhood pain and loss he'd suffered.

"You're crazy," old Peg said. It had an odd weight of conviction behind it. It was not the careless remark of somebody affectionately deriding a friend.

"Listen. Listen," Linus demanded. "I never had a birthday party when I was little."

"I don't want to hear about it. I don't want to hear you crying the blues. You think I haven't got things to complain about? I got things to cry about. I lost my husband in a car crash."

"Once at Christmas I asked one of the foster fathers I had—I don't remember which one—for a tricycle. I wanted it so bad. He made one out of an orange crate. It wasn't a real tricycle. Just an old crate and a board with skate wheels on it."

"My sons were killed in the war," old Peg said. "My daughter took sick with cancer and died when she was only thirty-five. Her husband moved away with my grandchild. I never did find out where."

"You hear what I said?" Linus demanded. "The damn thing was even too big for me. I couldn't make it go."

"Lost my house," Peg said angrily. "Took it away from me. I got sick. I couldn't get a job. Too old. Too old."

"It busted. That wooden scooter busted," Linus screamed. "Listen to what I'm saying to you. Listen to me."

"Too old, goddamn it to hell. You son of a bitch. You listen to me!"

He struck her in the face then with his fist.

She backed away from him, her hands held in front of her.

"It was you been stealing the pieces of my game."

"Shut up. Don't say anything more," Linus said as he stalked her.

"I read the papers. Don't think I don't read the papers. I know what you been doing with the pieces of my game."

He took the knife from his pocket then.

Finally Peg became afraid.

28.

"Who done it?" Eddie B asked.

"How would I know?" Linus answered.

"Your hands cold?" Eddie B asked.

"What are you asking me that for?"

"I never see you wear gloves before. I see you run around in zero weather with a sweater and scarf around your neck. I never see you wear gloves," Eddie B explained.

"Who gives a damn he wears gloves?" Bo Wango complained. He peered out of a huge turban made of rags and old pantyhose and a half dozen scarves. His eyes were like those of a ferret's or a water rat's.

"What we going to do?" Harry the Hangnail said.

"See she gets buried," Maud's Sister said.

"Who sees she does?" Eddie B asked.

They all looked to Linus.

"You were her best friend," Maud's Sister said.

"Who said that?" Linus wanted to know.

"Mumblety Peg said that. She always said that," Harry the Hangnail declared.

"She must have said it to me a million times," Maud's Sister agreed.

Linus turned his head away so that his acquaintances couldn't see the tears forming in his eyes.

"Was she Jewish?" Harry the Hangnail asked.

"Who the hell cares was she Jewish?" Maud's Sister yelped. "There ain't no anti-Semitism in the tunnels."

Harry didn't want to call her a liar, and he didn't think it was the right time to make an argument, so he let it go.

"I just mean that maybe she would want to be buried Orthodox."

"Maybe Reform," Eddie B said. "If she was any kind of Jew it would be Reform."

"She wasn't Jewish," Linus said.

"How do you know that?" Eddie B demanded.

"She ate bacon."

"So I eat bacon and I'm a Jew," Harry said. "These times eating bacon isn't a question of religion, it's a matter of survival."

"She was Lutheran," Linus said.

Having named it seemed to make it so.

"Did she ever say how she wanted it?" Maud's Sister asked.

"Wanted it?" Linus said.

"After she was gone. She say whether she wanted to be cremated or buried? She want a service in a church or just a few words at the graveside?"

"I don't think she cared."

"I'll wash her up and put a clean dress on her," Maud's Sister volunteered.

"You know how to do that?" Eddie B asked in some awe.

"I done it for my sister Maud, didn't I?"

131

"You touched her bare skin when she was dead?"

Maud's Sister looked at Eddie B in disgust, her eyebrows raised in a superior fashion.

"Get out of here and let me do it," she said.

The men shuffled to the door.

"Linus?" Maud's Sister called.

"Yeah?"

"We want right done by Mumblety Peg, don't we?"

"We want the best we can get."

"Campbell's on Madison Avenue has nice parlors."

"That's way up on Eighty-first. I don't think we could get her up there."

"Morris on Flatbush Avenue gives a nice funeral."

"My God, Maud's Sister, that's way the hell out in Brooklyn. We'd better stay in Manhattan."

"You're right. How about Redden's on West Fourteenth?"

"Wherever we leave her, they'll end up sending her over to the morgue on First Avenue."

"Maybe not," Maud's Sister said cheerfully. "Maybe not."

Besides Maud's Sister, Eddie B, Harry the Hangnail, Bo Wango, and Linus, there were thirteen other tunnel-dwellers in Mumblety Peg's funeral entourage. They started out from the tunnel where Peg had lived, pushing her along in the ancient wooden wheelchair that was Eddie B's dearest treasure. His home, his study, the bed in which he slept.

She was propped up, her shopping bags stuffed into the chair on either side of her. Her head was kept straight by three scarves wrapped around her neck and the heavy collar of a molting fur jacket. It served to conceal the handkerchief that tied up her jaw as well. There were dark glasses over her eyes, and a nylon square tied around her hair.

Her beloved games in their battered boxes were piled on her lap.

Maude's Sister and One-Eye carried candles at the head

132

of the procession, which threw grotesque shadows on the walls of the maze of Con Ed conduits they knew so well. Eddie B pushed the chair. Benny the Fool and Bo Wango carried two candles behind the parade of mourners. Linus walked beside old Peg, holding her cold, dead hand as though he were a doting relative.

They came to the mouth of a doorless opening in the station's lower level. The words "Burma Road" were scrawled above it, marking the main tunnel.

"This is as far as most of you can go," Linus said.

They all stood around shuffling their feet as though reluctant to give up the ceremony.

"Shouldn't the Reverend say his few words now, then?" Bo Wango asked.

The Reverend Moss took a small Bible, weathered and worn, from his back pocket. He cleared his throat as he thumbed through it seeking an appropriate text.

" 'Weep ye not for the dead, neither bemoan him—' "

"Her," Eddie B interrupted.

"What's that?" the Reverend asked, startled out of the mournful voice he had assumed.

"Her. Peg was a woman."

"Ah, ah, ah," Reverend Moss murmured to himself. " '—but weep sore for *her* that goeth away; for *she* shall return no more, and shall see *her* land no more.' "

There were a rattle of "Amens" that whispered away down the tunnels.

"Peg was a good woman. She didn't ask no favors," Maud's Sister said.

"She knew a funny story or two," Eddie B remarked.

Others of her acquaintances dropped little memories about her.

Linus didn't say anything at all. He acted as though his heart were too full of grief. In fact, he did regret Peg's death bitterly. However had it happened?

They all stood around shuffling their feet.

133

"That's it, then?" Linus said.

Still they didn't go away.

"Shouldn't we share out what she's got in the shopping bag?" Maud's Sister said. "No sense letting any stuff go to waste."

There was a murmur of general agreement about that.

Linus took the bags out of the chair. They gave him the man's overcoat Peg wore when it was very cold, because he'd lost his.

"The games stay with her," Linus said.

Bo Wango went to check that the way into the station was clear.

Eddie B and Linus wheeled Peg out onto the platform. They took the shuttle going to Times Square, leaving the tunnel-dwellers sharing out Peg's estate.

They took the IRT downtown and got out at 14th Street. Eddie B seemed reluctant to leave his chair with Linus.

"Don't worry, I'll bring it back," Linus said tightly.

Eddie B shied away from the cutting edge of his voice and took the next train out.

Linus was alone on the platform with Mumblety Peg. The world was empty in the small hours of the morning. He had the feeling that everyone had died and left him alone. He began to cry as he wheeled Peg to the farthest corner of the platform.

Across the tracks, under the shelter of a bench and covered with newspapers so that he seemed like nothing more than some crumpled pages, Willie the Walker was catching forty.

Willie was a street bum. In the summer he slept in the parks and cemeteries. In the spring and fall he sought doorways and furnace rooms, catching forty during the day and walking the streets during the night. Sometimes he spent what he had for a sleep on the mangy plush of a theater seat in an all-night house instead of on another pint of muscatel. Every winter he promised himself he'd go south to Florida,

134

but he never did. Instead he went down into the tunnels and stations. He knew some of that world's citizens. He knew Eddie B and recognized his chair when he opened one eye at the sound of sobbing in the hollow silence of the deserted station and saw somebody taking an old woman out of the chair and laying her down on the concrete. Willie started to straighten up, but thought better of it. He watched as Linus placed some boxes on Mumblety Peg's chest and crossed her hands on her stomach.

Linus took a soiled envelope from his pocket. It had a few dollars and some change in it. There was a penciled note that asked somebody to buy a bunch of flowers for the dead woman. He scattered some Chance cards from the Monopoly game on her.

He rolled the wheelchair off the platform onto the tracks. When the next train came in the chair would be busted up into matchsticks.

Linus went up the stairway to the street.

Willie the Walker would have robbed Peg's body except he was afraid of the dead. Instead, he went to find another place to sleep, grumbling to himself about people forcing him out of his usual sleeping place. He went up into the air. He was surprised to find it was not too cold. It smelled sweet.

29.

They sat around like a bunch of old card players who'd forgotten to bring a deck to the weekly game and didn't know what to do with themselves.

"Doc?" Posner said.

"Maybe I shouldn't," Mercado replied. "I'm batting zip up to now."

"So is everybody else."

"All right, then," Mercado said and straightened up in his chair, bringing his hands up and counting his fingers off again.

"This one was personal."

"Yeah?" Gertie said challengingly.

"I think he beat her up before he finished her with the knife. They had a fight. She made him mad."

"Only friends get that mad enough to kill," Malloy remarked.

"You know her, Malloy?" Posner asked.

"They called her Mumblety Peg. Yeah, I knew her."

"How well you know her?" Gertie asked.

"Ahhh," Malloy breathed and turned his head away impatiently as though all these questions were a waste of time. All this speculation a joke.

"You can't know the shopping bag ladies," he said. "You can't really know the people who live in the tunnels. They're going around the second time."

"What the hell does that mean?" Gertie rasped.

"They killed an old life back when," Malloy said. He closed his eyes as though he were infinitely weary.

"Do you know any of her friends?" Posner went on.

"Some of them. Know some of the people she might know. Not her friends really. They don't generally have many friends the way we'd call people friends. Might have one or two they travel with. Mostly they're loners."

Mercado smiled softly, regarding Malloy with soft, understanding eyes. The loner was talking about people being loners.

"Have you seen the stuff found on her?" Posner asked.

"Not yet."

"There was an envelope with four or five bucks in it."

"Yeah?"

"There was a note asking somebody to buy some flowers for her grave."

"I wonder was it the killer."

"Not likely," Limey said.

"Oh, I don't know," Malloy replied. "He killed a friend. He might be sorry."

"Or it could mean he doesn't care about anybody or anything any more," Mercado said.

They all looked at him as he counted out his hopes and fears on his fingers.

Funny habit, Malloy thought, as he sought the shadows of the room, hands in his pockets, feet planted wide as though fighting the sway of the subway cars.

"We're just supposing," Posner said, as though he were suddenly too tired to go on with it.

"That's all we can ever do," Mercado said. "Even after we catch the killers, and they tell us why they did what they did, it sounds like just supposing."

"What else was on her?" Malloy asked loudly, wanting to get away from speculation. Wanting something a little bit solid to hold on to.

"Boxes of games. All kinds," Posner said. He reached out and picked up the little pile of orange cards on his desk. He held them between his thumb and fingers as though he were ready to shuffle a deck and deal a hand. He set them down closer to Malloy, waiting for the cut.

"Any special marks on them?" Malloy asked without picking them up.

"Just scattered on her body."

Mercado reached out and picked up the top card.

"Chance," he said. "Last chance to catch me? Is that what he's saying?"

"Is he?" Malloy said and stood up. "Peg down at the morgue?"

Posner nodded.

"They going to bury her in Potter's Field?" Malloy asked.

"When the Medical Examiner releases her body, that's where she'll go. That's the provision the city makes for unknowns and indigents."

"They left her at Fourteenth," Malloy said.

"Yeah?" Posner responded.

"That's close to Redden's Mortuary."

"I know."

"You think they were hoping she'd get buried from there? Have a real funeral? You know?"

138

"That won't happen."

"I'll talk to Redden's. Maybe they'll do it for her. They owe me a favor."

"I'll mention it to the M E," Posner said.

"They won't do anything fancy," Malloy said, "but it'll be neat."

30.

Spring walked into New York City during the night the way it sometimes does, startling everyone into the belief that it was all going to be sunshine and roses for a while.

Joggers were stomping along the paths in Central Park all decked out in new running suits they'd been saving just for such a day. The steps of the Metropolitan Museum of Art were dotted with New Yorkers of all ages sticking their faces up toward the sun.

Irma sat there with her arms wrapped around her knees, head thrown back, eyes closed. Malloy was wearing his top-coat, hands in the pockets. He was squinting his eyes against the glare and looking wild, as though he were an animal trapped out in the open with nowhere to hide.

"Smell funny, Malloy?"

He sniffed.

140

"Yeah," he said in all innocence. "What is it?"

Irma looked at him and grinned.

"Fresh air," she said.

A newspaper came blowing along the street, marched up the shallow stairs, and plastered itself to Irma's leg. A cloud momentarily blocked some of the sun's light and heat. The breeze fluttered the paper against her calf.

She peeled it off and looked at it carelessly. The teaser above the headline said, "Monopoly Killer Still Stalking Subways." She looked at the date and handed it to Malloy.

"This is last Thursday's," she said.

"I remember that scare line," he said.

"Is it old news?" Irma asked hopefully. "I didn't see any notice on the front page this morning."

"It's not over," Malloy said.

"The cops put a lid on it?"

"They're not making any more gifts to Seagrave so he can sell papers."

"Has there been another killing?"

"Yeah."

He didn't seem ready to go on. Irma waited and finally he said, "It was different from the others."

"How different?"

"He killed somebody he knew. Somebody who was maybe even a friend."

"Ahhh," Irma said as though she had just suffered a deep pain.

They were silent for a while. They watched the people walking back and forth along the sidewalk, crossing the street, coming up into the museum.

"I got a letter from my sister," Irma said.

"Yeah, how is she?" Malloy asked brightly.

"I wrote to her last week."

"That's good. How is she?" he asked again.

"I asked her if there were any nursing jobs up there where she lives."

"In the woods?"

"Yeah, in the woods."

"What'd she say?" Malloy asked, not wanting to, but knowing it was what Irma wanted. She didn't want to be accused of bringing up the particular subject.

"She said there was work in the local hospital."

"Nurse with your credentials can always get work just about anywhere," Malloy said.

"Maybe, but my sister says there's an opening now."

"You'd like it up there," Malloy said helpfully.

"You liked it when we visited last year, didn't you? You liked it too."

"It was all right."

"I thought you liked it," Irma said, pleased by his admission.

"For a couple of days," he murmured, but Irma pretended not to hear that.

"Nice quiet town," she said. "Do you know they only had one assault in three years? One rape in four."

"It's a wonder they even need a hospital," Malloy said.

She preferred to let the remark go by. Preferred to treat it literally.

"They have their share of automobile wrecks. Mill accidents," she said.

"That's not so bad."

"Anything like that's bad, but it doesn't beat on you week after week," she said with a catch in her voice as though the pain of working Emergency was harder to handle when she wasn't actually in the ward. "They've got a police force," she added softly.

"I guess they do," Malloy said blandly.

"Sheriff's office for the county, too, I would imagine."

"That's usual."

The cloud passed over the sun again. A wind kicked up as cold as new winter. Malloy stood up.

"You forgetting, Irma?" he said.

142

"Forgetting what?"

"No regular police force could take me on even if they wanted to. I'm a cripple as far as real police work is concerned."

"Well, there are a lot of companies around there that use security."

"Hey, Irma," Malloy said, "you want me to be a night watchman?"

He started down the stairs and she went after him. She caught up with him on the pavement and grabbed his arm. She matched her stride to his.

31.

When Honker got a head cold it was a monument. His nose, when red and sore, became the center of his universe and, because of love, the center of Marsha's as well. He lay in bed looking out past the rain-streaked windowpane wondering if Malloy was down there in the musty-smelling tunnels riding round and round like a Biblical character in Hades, condemned to some bizarre, but telling, punishment.

He wanted to be with him. Not following along like an unwelcome shadow, but shoulder to shoulder with the man. He admired Malloy. When he sought the reasons why, it was easy to include the wounds suffered, the courage shown. But, more than those, there was a certain patience about Malloy that was Biblical and ancient. Malloy would not just endure, but prevail, through stubbornness if for no other reason.

Honker looked at the Monopoly game laid out on the bed

beside him. He'd hoped that some intuition would come to him by contemplating the signs and symbols the killer apparently found fascinating. They told him nothing. The killer's actions were as pointless, as random, as fate itself.

Linus wanted to be near Malloy too. It gave him an odd thrill to know that the big man who knew the tunnels nearly as well as Linus himself was riding the trains looking for him. Out of the millions in the city Malloy, and who knew how many cops, were thinking about *him*, giving up their days and nights for *him*, trying unsuccessfully to bring *him* down. He was somebody.

He tightened his folded arms, sensing the power in his thin arms. He looked around at the people riding in the subway car with him. If he wanted to, right now, he could change his seat, sidle up next to that old man sitting over there, nodding off over his newspaper, that fat woman over there staring off into space with blank, glazed eyes, that macho Spic with the slick hair and cruel eyes, licking his lips and trying to see through the clothes of every girl or woman who passed by. He could jolt them softly with his arm as the train swayed this way and that until he had a mind to slip the knife into them.

He smiled to himself. The Latino's stare landed on him. Linus stopped smiling and stared back. They played macho games with each other. Stop after stop went by. Neither one would break the stare. The spot between his eyes began to ache. Linus wanted to break it off, but the Puerto Rican wouldn't let him.

Linus had been fantasizing about killing one of the people on the train, but he didn't want to be forced into it by an unintended victim.

Linus dropped his eyes. He brought color to his cheeks. He glanced up and saw the swarthy face of his challenger break into a great triumphant smile. The man was about his own age, but built much more powerfully. He believed he'd faked Linus out, had him scared. It wasn't enough to

145

savor the victory from across the aisle. He got up. The swagger he affected was lost with his need to stay balanced with the swaying of the car. He sat down next to Linus and looked right into Linus's ear.

Linus got out at the next stop, hurrying along as though in fear. The Latino had nothing much to do. It would be a pleasure to run the rabbit a little bit, maybe back him into a corner, maybe steal his money or slap him in the mouth. He could smell the terror coming from the white boy's skin. It excited him. He'd have a story to tell.

Linus moved his pursuer around like a fish after a baited hook. He let the dude come close, but never close enough to make a move. He used other people as shields and diversions, stopped to buy a paper, looking fearful all the time. At 14th and Eighth Avenue he got the Canarsie Local. His hunter was right with him. Linus took him to Third Avenue and let the fool catch up with him in the men's room there.

The Puerto Rican never saw the knife that pierced his liver. The last thing he felt was Linus spitting in his face as he drew him in close with a hand clutching his shirt.

Linus reached into his pocket, looking for a card to drop on the body. He didn't have any. He couldn't remember if he'd simply lost them or left them with old Peg. Finally he knelt down beside the body and carved a question mark on the forehead. Then he relieved himself and washed his hands, enjoying the danger that someone might walk in on him with the corpse at his feet.

He went outside and sat on a bench, waiting for someone to find the body and call the police. Waiting for Malloy to arrive.

32.

It was more exciting than anything yet. Linus couldn't imagine why he hadn't done it before. Slipping the knife into somebody, then laying them out, dropping "clues" on them and reading about the scramble the cops were going through was nothing compared to hanging around nearby and watching them trying to act as though they knew what they were doing.

Only Malloy looked cool. Linus had to give him that. Sad, but cool, hands stuck in his pockets as though he knew damn well there wasn't a thing any of them could do about it.

Trains came in and out, unloading their passengers. It was near rush hour, and a lot of men tried to get into the toilets for a quick piss, but the cops kept them out. A lot of milling around. A lot of angry frowns and sharp remarks. So somebody had been knifed. Too bad. But what did that have to do with a guy's bladder when it needed relief? Linus could practically hear some of them saying things like that. He giggled to himself.

Malloy looked toward him as though he could hear Linus's laughter.

I know that kid, Malloy thought. Do I know that kid? A nice-looking boy with a brush of soft hair falling over his forehead. Clear eyes, looking a little tired and drawn right at the moment. There was a red mark like a hand print high up on one cheek, as though he'd been struck. Overcoat too big for him.

"Hey, Malloy," Seagrave said as he approached.

"What do you do, smell the corpses?" Malloy asked softly.

"We all do what we can do, Malloy," Seagrave said, his face set as if he feared he would cry if he didn't watch himself.

Malloy followed the reporter inside the washroom as though he meant to act as Seagrave's conscience.

The young Puerto Rican was sprawled out on his back, hands stiffly clawed about his middle where the knife had made itself felt deep in his guts. His eyes were open. Blood from the wound in his forehead had pooled in one-socket.

"Ugly goddamn business," Seagrave said.

"I didn't know you cared," Gertie said sarcastically, needling Seagrave for the way he did his job.

"He have a chance to defend himself?" Seagrave asked.

"You got eyes," Gertie said.

Seagrave took a step closer and squatted down.

"Looks like his knuckles are scraped," he said.

Malloy stepped out onto the platform again. The kid wasn't sitting on the bench any more.

Malloy closed his eyes and put his hand to his face so that

his thumb and first two fingers covered them. He tried to visualize where and when he'd seen the young man before.

Linus stood back against the wall on the far side of the tracks, having crossed over to the opposite platform while Malloy was inside the restroom. There was a projection that housed a tangle of cables and pipes, and a crew of workmen was repairing something in the guts of it. One was wheeling an acetylene rack into place. Another was probing around inside with a wrench, complaining under his breath about the long hours and the never-ending emergency calls.

Linus felt his heart beating so hard in his chest that it made it hard for him to breathe. The pounding echoed in his side where the wound was nearly healed, the stitches already dissolving away. The big idea had come to him as he sat on the bench covertly watching the Transit cop watching him.

One on one!

That was the game. The hell with piling up the anonymous dead. He'd bring down one of their own. Bring down the hunter and show them all who owned the city beneath the city.

He would stalk him slowly, carefully, savoring every moment of it. Maybe he'd present himself to Malloy often enough so that the cop would begin to think a lot about him, begin to wonder if he was the young man written about as "The Monopoly Killer." Maybe he'd stash the overcoat and show off his scarf.

The acetylene arc flashed. The flame burned orange and then blue as the feeder was adjusted. The workman shielded his eyes with a pair of goggles and set the point of flame to the part needing repair. Sparks flew. They drew the attention of Malloy.

He saw the young man standing in the shadows created by the service pillar protruding from the wall, the sparks giving a hellish cast to his soft features, which were so oddly cruel.

149

Linus knew he'd been seen. He came out of hiding altogether. Keeping his eyes on Malloy's he walked over to the staircase that would lead to the upper level and another staircase that would bring him back to the platform where Malloy was beginning to walk in order to get closer to Linus.

Malloy was waiting for Linus as he came down the staircase. The overcoat was off, draped over his arm, the scarf could be plainly seen around his shoulders. His hand held the knife, concealed by the folds of the coat. He was grinning. Malloy couldn't yet see that from the angle of his view.

Linus took another step. A train rushed into the station, its brakes wailing. A crush of people poured out. Malloy was shouldered aside, but he could still see Linus's legs, standing still, waiting for the flood of humanity to go around him.

There was a sudden sense of vacuum, a curious silence like a held breath. Then the explosion roared out. The acetylene had touched off a pocket of escaping gas.

Just in front of him, a woman was thrown against the wall with such force that her head was smashed against the white tiles and split open from temple to jaw. A big man was knocked to his knees, his eyeglasses smashed, the bits of glass thrown into his eyes. Malloy, himself, was spun around and thrown against the backs and legs of half a dozen people climbing the stairs, bringing them down like so many tenpins.

From Linus's point of view it was as though a giant hand had slapped the people who had been, but a moment before, carelessly jostling him aside as they hurried to get up and out of the tunnels into the fresh air and the way home. Facing the force of the explosion as he was, the heavy column of expanding air, driven through every aperture like water constricted in narrow gorges, pushed against his chest and knocked him into a sitting position on the steps.

Below him, he could see Malloy struggling to his feet. The

150

curious silence returned and held for a long moment, and then breaking glass, falling objects, and the screams of men and women shattered it, flying like knife points into the pain behind his eyes. Malloy's hand was to his own eyes. When he took it away there was blood on it. He stared at it for a moment, then, reaching for a handkerchief, wiped it off. He touched himself, discovering that he had no cuts. The blood belonged to someone else. He went to one knee and began to untangle the confusion of bodies.

A moment later Linus was beside him. The knife was still in his hand, still concealed in the folds of the overcoat. He quickly closed the blade and stuffed the knife into the pocket of the coat, then put it on, covering the scarf.

Together he and Malloy began to lift up a woman whose neck appeared to be broken.

33.

Later that day, when the first newspapers hit the street, the dry statistics would give one impression of what had occurred. Five dead and seventy-three injured. A big enough disaster compared to subway disasters of the past. Not nearly as bad as the Malbone Street wreck on the old BRT back in 1918. Just a little worse than the Roosevelt Avenue crash in 1970.

On the scene, at the time, there were no statistics, just people in terrible danger and pain.

Gertie, Limey, Posner, and a dozen uniforms came barreling out of the washroom. That gave them an edge on the rescue operation. By the time the first ambulance crews had arrived the police officers had already sorted out a good deal of the shambles the explosion had created. The train in the station had been rocked off the tracks. The two center cars were lying on the roadbed, still on their wheels, but heeled over like ships running into the wind, their couplings twisted and split apart.

There were people inside cut by the flying glass. One man was dead, speared through the throat by a flying shard of a window. His blood was splashed on the sides of the car inside like another swipe of graffiti. A woman was screaming in the gloom inside one of the cars with the steady pulse of a beating heart.

Malloy and Linus got the woman with the twisted neck laid out on the platform. Seagrave came up behind them, looking alert and happy, like a hunting dog doing what it was born to do. He had a 35 mm. automatic-exposure, automatic focus camera in his hand. He pointed it at Linus and Malloy bending over the woman and triggered the flash.

Malloy turned to see the source of the blinding light and saw Seagrave there. Their eyes met for a moment. Malloy's made no judgment.

When he turned back to the victim, Linus was gently placing a folded-up scarf under her head. It was already red with blood. He smiled nervously at Malloy, and then they moved off together like buddy corpsmen moving through the casualties of battle.

They stooped to examine a girl of thirteen or fourteen who was sitting on the ground, her back against the tiles, staring straight ahead and shivering like a wet dog. Linus took her up and carried her to the bench nearby. He spread the overcoat and wrapped it around her thin shoulders. Then he asked a man standing aside to stay with her as Seagrave snapped another picture.

There was noise enough to prevent much intelligible exchange of conversation or instruction. Cops were bellowing out commands and assurances, telling everyone that things were all right, even as they bled. A few of the cops were injured as well. The steam lines on the trains had been snapped. The hissing sounded like that of a thousand snakes

153

in a pit. People were moaning. But above it all the keening cry of the woman trapped somewhere in the car rose up as the sharpest expression of human pain and anguish.

Then, belatedly, the lights in the station went out. The emergency batteries in the cars illuminated the interiors of them as people still struggled to get out. The policemen turned on their flashlights, pointing the beams here and there, lighting up the faces of the injured and the rescuers. The clouds of steam made pretty patterns in the cavern.

Seagrave's camera flashed blue in the semi-dark.

Malloy and Linus, without speaking to each other, went into the car where the woman cried out monotonously, lost to her shock and pain. They made their way back to the end, where they saw her lying underneath the wreckage of the seats. Linus went down on his belly and crawled underneath a twisted support to tell her that she'd been found.

Malloy began to pull at the seat's framework. The pitch and intensity of the woman's cry changed, grew more strident.

"I see what's got her," Linus said.

"Is she pinned or stabbed through?" Malloy asked.

"The weight of it's just lying on top of her. I think she'll have to stand it when we lift up on the seats."

"Shall I pull up on this bar?" Malloy asked, touching the part of the frame closest to the woman, underneath the cushion beyond his view.

"Wait. Let me get under it. I think I'm skinny enough," Linus said. He snaked his way under the steel bars. He got his shoulders and back under the angle of the one leaning directly on the woman's twisted legs.

"I think if you pull up at a forty-five degree angle when I start to raise up, we can get her out," Linus said.

"Go for it, kid," Malloy answered and patted the thin ankle that was protruding out of the wreckage.

Linus grit his teeth. He suddenly thought about the wound in his side. It was pretty well healed up, but this strain

154

could easily do him some harm. He hesitated for a moment, then felt Malloy pat his ankle again, urging him on. They were working together. They needed each other to do this thing they'd set out to do.

Linus started to lift up, grunting, "Now," as he did so.

Malloy heaved on the seat bars. The woman screamed sharply and then stopped as though cut off at the throat. She'd fainted. Malloy knew that was the best thing.

In two minutes more they had her out. Malloy lifted her up in his arms and took her out onto the platform, with Linus leading the way, just as the lights came on.

Seagrave got that picture, too.

After Malloy had given the woman over to the care of an ambulance crew, he turned to Linus and grinned.

"We did all right," he said.

Linus grinned back.

"You gave away your coat," Malloy said.

"I don't live far," Linus replied. "I won't get cold."

"I was looking at you just before the tunnel blew."

"I know."

"Have we met?"

"I don't think so."

"I'm down in the subways a lot."

"Me too," Linus said.

They regarded each other silently for a time, then Malloy stuck out his hand and smiled.

"We did all right," he said again.

Linus shook his hand. Then he turned away, leaving Malloy with the thought that he knew Linus from somewhere, but he was damned if he could remember.

The story on the 14th Street explosion took up the whole front page of Seagrave's paper. His byline was prominent. His carping about the "Monopoly Killings" took no space in the edition at all for a change. The eyewitness account took up much of the space left over after the headline. His photos, one of Malloy and Linus among them, took up the rest.

About an hour after the paper hit the street, Mrs. Roth, the quiet little woman who'd remembered that the young man who helped carry her friend, Sadie, off the train was the same one who'd been sitting next to her, tracked Malloy down on the telephone.

"Mr. Malloy," she said, after she'd identified herself, "do you remember that I recalled the strange thing about that boy?"

"Yes, I do," Malloy replied.

"Well, I've seen him again."

In an instant Malloy could almost have told her exactly what she was about to say. He saw the face of the kid who'd played hero at the disaster. Saw the face at Grand Concourse, and other stations along the lines, smiling and blushing, and doing his dog and pony act for quarters until he spotted Malloy out of the corner of his eye and took off, thinking he'd escaped identification by a cop.

"Yes, ma'am?" Malloy said.

"In the paper. On the front page of this evening's paper. He was with you."

Sure. Why not? The crazy "Monopoly Killer" liked playing games. Liked the excitement of teasing the cops. Like a junkie, though, he needed a bigger and bigger fix. More excitement, more danger, and more adrenaline.

"Thank you, Mrs. Roth," Malloy said, and hung up the phone.

34.

Sometimes Eddie B forgot why he was called that. Forgot what the B stood for. Other times he knew it was the initial of his last name, Benson. Edward Benson had been his name, and he'd been married to a pleasant enough woman who had grown away from him as he had grown away from her. There had been three daughters. One in her teens, the others nearly so, when last he saw them. They would always remain that way in his memory, when it functioned.

Edward Benson had been a securities analyst for a bank in Elmira, New York. Successful. Two cars. Big house. Country club membership. All of that.

His story was so commonplace as to be pitiful, if not trivial.

"The bottle done me in," he sometimes said, as though he'd lost good grammar along with everything else. As though speaking properly might remind him too painfully of who he'd once been.

They call the condition he suffered "wet brain." It's as bad and as foolish as it sounds.

He lay in the corner of a tunnel trying to make himself small. He had been sleeping worse than usual of late, like a man who has been forced by misadventure to sleep in a strange bed. He missed his wheelchair terribly. It had been more than a place to rest. It had been his home.

Linus had claimed the chair had just skittered away like something alive while he was struggling to get Peg out of it and laid out on the station platform. He'd looked straight into Eddie B's eyes while he told the lie. Eddie B knew that Linus was one of the mean ones who prowled the tunnel even if he did look like a schoolboy and smiled in that shy way he had.

A matchhead of rage flared inside his chest. It startled him, as a sour belch would do. He sat straight up and examined the feeling that was pinwheeling around inside his chest, threatening his heart and nighttime digestion. Eddie B was not often pushed to anger. It was an unfamiliar but not altogether unpleasant feeling. The energy it gave him brought him to his feet, and he shuffled off down the tunnel looking for the company of people.

He passed by Bo Wango and Maud's Sister. Their heads were close together. They were looking into each other's eyes and grinning foolishly. Eddie B wondered what it could be about. He remembered vaguely that people kissed and mentioned feelings called love. He laughed out loud. It was too funny to think of those two kissing and saying such things to each other, whispering tenderness into ears caked with grime.

"Foolish, foolish fools," he crooned and threw his head back so that his laughter would get lost in the roof of the tunnel as he passed the niches and doorways full of shadows. He didn't even see Linus sitting in one of them.

Eddie B took the train to Union Square, where Tony served up pepper sandwiches and chemical drinks the color of bright paint.

"How you doing, Eddie B?" Tony greeted the night roamer.

"Okay. What you doing opened?"

"It's not that late. I'll get some ten o'clock action. What the hell. It's a buck."

Eddie B looked around as though counting the people that weren't there.

"Where's your throne?" Tony asked. "Where's your wheels?"

"Got busted," Eddie said.

"How the hell that happen?"

"Some son of a bitch . . ." Eddie B started to scream, but caught himself. "Never mind."

"Well, how'd it happen?" Tony insisted.

"Accident. Rolled off the platform over on Fourteenth west and the train smashed it up."

"I'll be a son of a bitch," Tony said, awed by the picture served up by his imagination.

"Yeah," Eddie B mourned.

"That's too damn bad. You want something, Eddie B?"

"No."

"Got no coin?"

Eddie B shook his head.

"Ah, hell, I can do you an orange on the house."

Eddie climbed up on a stool.

"Can you make it a grape?"

"Sure, why the hell not?" Tony said, feeling big about the whole thing. He filled up a cardboard cup with cracked ice and poured purple sweetness on top.

Eddie B got off the stool and picked the cup up in both hands. He buried his nose in the stuff and drank almost all of it down in one long go.

"Thirsty, huh?" Tony said.

"Sometimes I get so goddamn thirsty in the middle of the night I could cry," Eddie B confided. "It's the goddamn steam heat. Dries out the sinuses. Dries out the throat."

"You ought to get a thermos," Tony said.

"What?"

"Ought to get yourself a thermos or a plastic bottle. Keep some water in it, you know? No reason to go thirsty in the middle of the night."

Eddie B thought about that. It was a little too much for him. He finished the grape drink and carefully put the cup back on the counter. Then he reached in his pocket and put down a dirty envelope next to it.

"What's that?" Tony asked. "You want I should toss it in the trash with the cup?"

"No. Don't do that. It's a note for somebody."

"Yeah, who?"

"You know Malloy, the subway cop?"

"Everybody knows Malloy," Tony smiled.

"Will you give this to him?"

Tony picked the envelope up by the corner.

"How'd you get it so dirty?"

"I found it in the street," Eddie B confessed. "And I've been carrying it around for a while."

"You sure you want to give this to Malloy?"

"Yeah, I'm sure."

"What's in it? What's it say?"

Eddie B frowned. He was too polite or too timid to tell the counterman that it was none of his business. Tony shrugged as a couple of teenagers came walking up to the counter. They were damp from the drizzle that threatened another storm.

"What's it my business. Sure, Eddie B. I'll give it to him next time I see him," Tony said, and put the note by the register.

He turned to the customers and took their orders. Eddie B

160

hesitated, wondering why it was that he and Tony were having a conversation one minute and he was being closed out the next. Tony was dishing up two sandwiches and pouring drinks and not even paying Eddie B any attention any more.

"Thanks for the grape," he said, starting to walk away.

"I'll see Malloy gets it," Tony said, and waved, but didn't even look at Eddie B.

Eddie B walked down to the exit. He shuffled along the pedestrian tunnel, then popped through a service door into a Con Ed conduit. He coughed and smiled as the echo came back to keep him company.

He didn't hear the slightest scraping of a foot. All of a sudden Linus was there like an evil magician appearing out of the tunnel wall, grinning and dangerous. Eddie B screamed out and jumped a foot.

"Jesus Christ, Linus," he whimpered. "You scared the bejeesus out of me."

"I did, huh?" Linus grinned. "I really scared you?"

"Jumping out at me that way."

"What way?" Linus asked innocently, and then leaped into the air, coming down crouching, arms extended, hands clawed. "Bam! Bam!" he shouted.

Eddie B cried out again and that seemed to satisfy Linus for the moment. He moved beside the smaller man and threw his arm around Eddie B's shoulders, pulling him in close, making him walk along.

"Where you going?" he asked in the same way Eddie B always asked the question.

"Sixth Avenue subway," Eddie B said.

"Yeah?"

"Going uptown."

"What for?"

"I don't know."

"Looking for your chair?"

161

"No," Eddie B replied after some hesitation. He sensed that Linus was laying some sort of trap for him, but he couldn't identify the nature of the danger he smelled.

"How come? I never see you without your chair. Where's your chair?"

Eddie B looked up into Linus's face in real surprise.

"You know," he said.

"What do I know?" Linus taunted.

"You know I ain't got the chair any more."

"How come?"

"You know."

"Why the hell you keep telling me I know when I don't know?" Linus suddenly raged.

"You never brung it back to me," Eddie B screeched.

Linus stopped short, forcing Eddie B to stop as well. His hand tightened on the little man's shoulder.

"You putting me on?" Linus threatened.

"You said you'd bring it back to me. You promised, but you never did," Eddie B whined. Tears were welling up in his eyes, threatening his safety.

"Sure I did, Eddie B. I brought it back just like I promised," Linus said.

Eddie B shook his head furiously, the tears flying loose in a glittering spatter.

"You never did."

Linus stared at him for a long while. Eddie B grew terrified under the steady regard. It caused a flash of memory to flood his belly and grip his heart. When he'd been a small boy someone had taken him to the slaughter house. The huge man who poleaxed the steers as they walked out on the killing floor was laughing and joking with some of the other workers. Then a bell rang and an old cow came racketing through the chute. The man hefted the heavy killing tool in his two hands and stared at the animal. Stared right between its eyes as Linus was doing to him now.

162

"That why you're pissed off at me?" Linus asked very softly.

"I never said I was," Eddie B said hurriedly.

"You putting me on again?" Linus grated. "You saying you're not mad at me?"

"No, no. I ain't."

"Ain't what?"

"Ain't mad at you."

"What a liar you are. What a terrible liar you are."

"I'm not."

"Yes you are. If you're not pissed off at me why're you sending for the cops?"

"Whatever give you that idea?" Eddie B whispered. It was like a scream, thin and shrill, the words barely getting past his throat, which felt as though it were closing up on him.

"That envelope you slipped to Tony at the sandwich counter," Linus reminded him.

"I didn't give Tony no letter. What would I want to give Tony a letter for?"

"Who said anything about a letter? I said an envelope. There's all kinds of envelopes."

"I didn't give him no envelope."

"Oh, what a liar you are," Linus accused again. "You gave Tony a note for the cops because I had an accident and your chair got busted."

"I didn't do no such thing," Eddie B continued to protest.

Linus backed away, looked down at the ground, and shuffled his feet. He brushed the fan of hair away from his forehead.

"Oh, yeah," he said casually as though accepting what Eddie B was saying. "What was in the envelope then?"

"Nothing."

"Just an empty envelope. You going crazy handing out empty envelopes?" Linus went on patiently, gently, his

163

voice growing soft and soothing as he smiled down at Eddie B. "What was in it?"

"Just a message."

"To who?"

Suddenly inspired, Eddie B lit up and said, "Tony."

"Oh, my. You sending notes to young men? You sending love letters to young Italian boys? You turning queer in your old age?"

"No!"

"What then?"

"Just saying thanks," Eddie B improvised madly.

"What for?"

Jesus, Eddie B thought, won't he let it go? Won't he ever let me alone? He felt his skin crawl, wanting to run away.

"He gives me free grape drinks. Sometimes he gives me a pepper sandwich. Sometimes a hot dog."

Linus grew deadly still. From far above there was a rumbling. Eddie B lifted his head.

"Going to rain up there," he said, trying a conversational diversion.

Linus's hand and arm snaked out. He caught Eddie B by the shirt and drove him up against the sweating concrete of the tunnel walls.

"Oh, Jesus!" Eddie B cried out.

"Yeah, yeah, yeah. You better pray."

"What are you going to do?" Eddie B asked fearfully.

"What would you do to a rat? To a sewer rat?"

Eddie B started to say something, anything to placate Linus, but the younger man slammed him up against the wall again, knocking the breath from him.

"You kill a rat," he spit out through his clenched teeth. The spittle sprayed Eddie B. He closed his eyes. He couldn't manage to turn away.

"You step on its head. You step on its head," Linus went on softly. "You stomp on it and squash its guts."

Eddie B began to moan deep in his chest.

"Who were you ratting to, Eddie B?" Linus asked.

"The subway cop."

"Malloy."

"Yeah."

"What did you tell him?"

"Nothing."

"Eddie B," Linus said warningly, the name lifting at the end.

"I just asked him to meet me," Eddie B insisted.

"Where?"

"The church."

"Which one?"

"St. Luke's Chapel on Hudson Street."

"What for? What were you going to tell him?"

There was something in Linus's expression that convinced Eddie B that the kid would know if he dared to lie.

"I was going to tell him you busted my chair."

Linus's face seemed to grow small, as though he'd bitten into a lemon, then it expanded, his mouth turning up at the corners. Then he was laughing uproariously, almost out of control, but never taking his clutch off Eddie B's shirt front.

"Ah, Jesus," Linus said when his laughter stilled. "You're a pistol, Eddie B." Then the nice face of laughter was wiped away just like that, a match going out.

"Now you tell me when you asked to meet with this cop," Linus demanded.

"I told him I'd be there just around dark every night this week till he come."

"You know what, Eddie B?" Linus prompted.

"What?"

"I think you're just nuts enough to put the cops on me over that goddamn old rotten chair of yours."

"You shouldn't of busted it," Eddie B started to say, determined to state the justice of his case.

165

Linus shook him like a rag.

"Shut up. Maybe that's all you want to tell Malloy. Maybe that's all. But maybe you want to tell him something else."

The thunder rumbled overhead again. Eddie B wished desperately that he were up on the street, even if he had to get soaking wet. When he was a little kid he used to love splashing through the rain running down the gutters. He remembered that. Then his eye caught the motion as Linus reached into his pocket and took out the knife.

"Maybe you want to tell Malloy I killed Peg," Linus said, but his voice didn't mask the snick of the blade springing free. "Maybe that's what you really want to do, and I can't let you do that."

"Nooo," Eddie moaned, wanting to protest sharply, but managing no more than a prayer.

"I can't let you do that," Linus said again, his voice straining as he prepared for the effort of stabbing Eddie B to death. His arm drew back. Eddie B struggled. His cheek scraped against the rough concrete sealing the rim of a drain in the wall. A great gush of dirty water burst from the end of the pipe. Eddie B broke free in that single startled moment when Linus loosened his grip. He went running off down the tunnel. Linus watched him go as he stood in the rush of water before it slowed to a trickle. He laughed softly.

"Oh, just you wait, Eddie B. I can get you any time. Just you wait, Eddie B."

166

35.

Malloy made his rounds. He was more faithful about walking his beat than any cop up on the streets. It was still drizzling fitfully up above. Except for the smell of wet wool, the subway stations were almost cozy.

Honker was glad that Malloy was staying below, making the changes from line to line through the pedestrian tunnels at selected stops. His cold was better, but not perfect. He felt the end of his nose with all his fingers. It was still very sore.

Malloy went into a shoe repair shop.

"How's it hangin', Malloy?" the shopkeeper greeted him.

"Heavy. How's by you?"

"Can't complain."

"My shoes ready?" Malloy asked.

"What's today?"

"Tuesday."

"What day I tell you they'd be ready?"

"Tuesday."

The old Italian grinned. "So call me a liar. Tomorrow. They'll be ready tomorrow."

"See anything?" Malloy asked.

"What am I looking for?"

"A kid who pulls the schoolboy trick for subway fare."

Malloy took a blowup of the section of the photograph taken at the scene of the disaster and printed in the paper. He gave it to the shoemaker to examine. The old man peered at it, then looked up and grinned.

"You kidding me?" he said. "Even with perfect eyes I couldn't tell much from this picture of the side of a face with a scarf covering it almost to the nose. What else can you tell me? Where does he work his act?"

"I think I've seen him at Queensboro Plaza. Penn Station. Maybe the Grand Concourse."

"Malloy, I live out in Bay Ridge. From here to there I ride the train. Everything in between is a foreign country to me. Once my wife made me go visit some distant relatives in the Bronx. I got sick on the water. What can I tell you?"

"Shoes ready tomorrow?" Malloy said.

"Whenever."

Malloy walked on with the steady flat-footed stride of the beat cop, hands in his pockets, head pulled into his collar, but his eyes alert.

He talked to this one and that, change-makers, news vendors, the workers in fancy shops in the underground concourses. He dropped a buck in the shaker of a nun who was no nun.

A blind man would know the girl he stopped to chat with was a hooker. His nose would tell him. Honker knew that her perfume could stun an ox. He'd be on his knees if it wasn't for the plugs created by his cold even though he was across the tracks. He crossed on over by the stairways.

168

When he got on the other side he was behind Malloy, who was smiling down into the girl's face.

"You moving uptown again, Margie?" Malloy asked.

"A change of scene is nice."

"That all?"

"Well . . ." Margie hesitated.

"Maybaum getting on your case again?" Malloy sympathized.

"Son of a bitch wants freebies."

"I thought you were already giving him samples. Price of doing business."

"Well, I was."

"He want something else?"

"I did."

"You wanted him to pay?" Malloy said in startled disbelief.

"No. Nothing like that."

"Then he wanted money?"

She shook her head, sending out waves of scent. Malloy backed up a pace.

"He promised to take me to Atlantic City one weekend. To the casinos," Margie complained.

"How the hell is he going to get away from his wife for a whole weekend?" Malloy wanted to know.

"Well, he manages to hide an afternoon or a night here and there, don't he?" Margie said reasonably.

"But a whole weekend can be tough."

"He shouldn't make promises he can't keep then," Margie pouted.

"You should know better than to believe anything an undercover cop tells you."

"He says he loves me."

"That's what I mean," Malloy said.

"You know a kid works the broke student gag?" he went on.

"Know a couple."

"This one is tall, thin, wears a scarf a lot. Hair falls in his eyes."

"Good-looking?"

"I'd say so."

"But bad eyes," Margie nodded. "I don't know him. I mean I know who you're talking about. I've seen him around. But I don't know him, you know?"

"If you see him, will you leave a call with me?" Malloy said, handing over one of his badly printed cards.

Margie grinned, showing a gray tooth that needed attention.

"Your home number here, Malloy?"

"No, but they'll get me any hour of the day or night."

"A girl gets lonely sometimes," Margie teased.

"You know what would happen," he said.

"Irma would put me in the hospital, then take good care of me," Margie laughed.

"You'll keep an eye out for this kid?" Malloy asked, having played the game that made Margie feel good.

"Sure. Is it bad?"

"As bad as it can be. He killed one of our own."

"Ahh, Jesus," Margie said softly.

Malloy bent down and kissed her cheek.

It went that way for a couple of hours, Malloy going from place to place all over the system, talking to everyone, letting it be known that he was bearing down on the hunt. That it was something special and nothing they should play "I don't want to get involved" about.

Honker could easily tell that Malloy wasn't just running blind any more. He wasn't beating the bushes, but was sending out the word, stalking someone known to him. It didn't take a big brain to know that whatever Malloy knew hadn't been shared with the cops yet. Maybe Malloy was afraid of making another mistake, like the one they'd made backing that civilian to the wall. Maybe he just wanted to handle it his own way.

170

That was all to the good as far as Honker was concerned. He knew who he meant to stick to. When Malloy flushed the game, he, Honker, would help make the collar and there'd be no extra dicks or uniforms around to share the credit.

Honker began to feel worse and wanted to go home. He had instincts too, and they told him Malloy wasn't going to have any luck tonight. He'd follow Malloy one more stop and that would be that.

At the sandwich stand he watched Malloy talking to Tony and saw the counterman hand over an envelope. Malloy read it, looked at his watch, and then hurried off as though he were really going somewhere.

36.

The "Monopoly" story was practically dead in the water.

You can't make a tired horse run past a certain point no matter how hard you beat him. To capture the attention of the public there had to be fresh disclosures, new outrages.

Seagrave had run out of things to say, fingers to point, accusations to be cast, and failures to be condemned. He needed an angle. Running stories were not that easy to come by, and he wanted to get all the mileage he could out of this one. He was growing stale, in danger of drying up. The ideas came harder, the words slipped like cold molasses from his fingertips.

He thought he might be able to take a new perspective on it if he could get an interview with the Transit cop, Malloy, but Martin had told him in no uncertain terms that

Seagrave was no longer in Malloy's favor. At least not for now. And not for a while.

He expected he'd get no more, probably less, from the detectives assigned from Manhattan South. In fact there were already strong indicators that they were capping the investigation, in preparation for filing it altogether. They were taking the position that the Latino found in the public john with the mark carved on his face had nothing to do with the "Monopoly Killer." They claimed it to be a gang killing plain and simple.

Seagrave had the feeling there was something else, something prior, he wasn't being told about.

Seagrave's charm wasn't working on Will Ory. Neither was the twenty woven through the columnist's fingers. He added another twenty to the first, smoothing out both bills and pairing them face up.

"You keep doing that, I'll have to charge you with trying to bribe an officer," Ory said.

"You got it all wrong, Ory; I'm not trying to pay you for any classified information," Seagrave said. "I don't want to have a peek at anything."

"Nothing to peek at," Ory said.

"Nothing having to do with what?" Seagrave asked very casually.

"To do with the Monopoly killings," Ory said in a voice showing the offense he felt that Seagrave should take him for a fool. He knew damn well what the newspaperman was after.

"Did I ask you anything about that?" Seagrave asked smoothly.

"Well, no," Ory replied doubtfully.

"I mean if there's anything going on with that geek, don't you think the public out there has a right to know about it? Has a right to defend itself?"

173

"Jesus, I don't know. I guess so."

"You're damn right it has," Seagrave said with an air of finality. "You're a servant of the public, aren't you?"

"What do you mean?"

"I mean, don't they call you a servant of the people? That's what a cop is. We're both servants of the people, right?"

"I guess so. Yeah."

"All I want to do is let the people know if they're safe from this crazy that's running through the subway system killing everybody he sets eyes on."

The outrageous exaggeration drew no criticism from Ory. Seagrave was in full flight, and the old cop was soaring right along with him, buying the whole store.

"Maybe the killer's dead himself?" Seagrave said.

"Not that I know of."

"Me neither. But maybe. Just maybe he fell under a train. What do you think?"

Ory shrugged.

"Just maybe he fell under a train," Seagrave repeated, watching Ory out of the corners of his eyes. "Why else would he just disappear from sight the way he has?"

"He ain't disappeared," Ory said.

"No kidding? How do you know? How can you be sure of that?"

"We're sure. Pretty sure."

"That's what I want to know. I mean the people got a right to know if they're not safe in the trains, right."

"We're sure."

"You figure him for that toilet killing at the explosion?"

Ory nearly tripped over his own tongue trying to say yes and no at the same time. "That was gang," he finally said.

"Well, all right, then," Seagrave said with relief, as though they'd both gotten through some sort of ordeal together. "Now there's no reason why you can't tell me who else he's killed."

174

"Now I'm not certain he's the one who done it," Ory warned.

"Just give me what they think," Seagrave said.

"A shopping bag lady got it."

"Which one?"

"They called her Mumblety Peg."

Seagrave looked up at the ceiling, trying to remember which one of so many she was.

"Got it," he said. He handed over one of the twenties.

"Tell me what was found on her."

"Some games."

"What else?"

"Some Chance cards from a Monopoly set."

Seagrave pushed the other twenty over with a skinny finger.

"For Christ's sake, don't quote me," Ory pleaded, suddenly aware that he'd spilled his guts again. Jesus Christ, he thought, Seagrave's got a way with him. How come he can always worm it out of me? He tucked the two twenties into his pocket.

"Unknown sources," Seagrave said. "Unknown sources."

Seagrave knew just about everybody in the city. That is to say he knew at least one of every race, creed, color, sex, religion, and political persuasion.

He knew his way around the ball park, the jailhouses, the hospitals, the morgue, the theaters, the night clubs; and he thought he knew his way around the tunnels. He didn't. He only knew a few of the avenues and boulevards, the main ones, not the alleys and the hidden lanes that were as plentiful under the ground as they were above.

But he did know enough to start in the tunnels underneath Grand Central and the blocks around it. That is where most of the buildings are heated by the steam generated by the power plant. That is where the refugees from the straight world earn their visas into the tunnels. It costs to travel anywhere.

A green finnif was Seagrave's ticket. He snapped the five dollar bill in front of the nose of Ralphie Potato, a nose that had been mashed by one fist too many and fried by one bottle more than enough. Ralphie Potato stood on the border, one foot in each world, making a buck where he could.

"Who you want pounded?" Ralphie asked.

"What does that buy me?"

"The price of everything is going up."

"I know it."

"For a fiver I'll bust somebody's finger. The little one."

"How much for a ten?" Seagrave bargained.

"Bust a thumb," Ralphie said.

Seagrave handed over another five.

"I'm not mad at anybody," he said.

"Then what do you want?" Ralphie wondered.

"Just a walk along the avenue."

"Which avenue?"

"The one that goes to Mumblety Peg's."

Ralphie took a step backwards and half raised his hands as though ready to ward off a couple of jabs.

"Ain't you heard?" he asked.

"I know, she's dead," Seagrave said.

"So?"

"I figure she rates a feature column. I figure a lady who lives in the tunnels and carries her life around in a shopping bag, asking no favors from anybody, has got a right to a little consideration. Got a right to a little notice. It's not right she should die with nobody to say a few words."

"The Reverend Moss said a few words."

"A few printed words. It's not right she should die and not even a whisper up on the streets."

"She didn't die, she was killed," Ralphie Potato said,

176

describing a difference that was very real to him. Most of the tunnel-dwellers dreamed about dying in a real bed the way square citizens thought of going without pain.

"I know that, too," Seagrave said. "Hey, Ralphie Potato, I'm not out to hurt her, or her memory."

"I wasn't a pal, you know," Ralphie pointed out. "The best I can do, maybe, is take you to somebody who knows the neighborhood where she used to live."

They entered the tunnels at the entrance marked "Burma Road." Seagrave wondered at the origin of it, but all Ralphie Potato could say was that it was christened way back when at the end of the Second World War.

"I was in it, do you know?" he boasted.

"The army?"

"Yeah, the army. Special Services. You know I was a fighter? Golden Gloves champion from New Jersey."

"Yeah, I know, Ralphie Potato," Seagrave said.

They walked shoulder to shoulder along the Con Ed tunnel as Ralphie remembered the past and the promising young man he once was.

"Turned pro after the war. Had fifteen fights. Lost one of them. The last one. Young Wiley knocked me out. Fell like a stone they tell me. Hit my head. Things were never the same."

"I'm sorry," Seagrave apologized for fate.

"Hell, what for? I was never that much good anyhow. It was just as well I lost that way. Just as well I got hurt bad enough never to fight again. My God, I got out when the getting was good."

Seagrave glanced at Ralphie Potato. The punch-drunk ex-fighter was grinning from ear to ear, glad to have escaped misfortune so narrowly.

"Here," he said and ducked into a smaller tunnel running off to the side. It was hotter than the larger one. Seagrave took off his coat and threw it over one shoulder. There were

177

the sounds of rats, cohabitants with men in the city within a city.

At the joining of two main thoroughfares Bo Wango sat on his haunches, his wares spread out on a piece of blanket at his feet. He was one of only a few underground vendors. His appearance was against any success as a beggar, so bizarre that he became the harassed quarry of even the cops who knew him well.

"Good Christ, you'll give the subways a bad name, Bo Wango. Get the hell back into your hole," they'd say and laugh when he scurried away, his head bobbing like some great mushroom, wreathed in discarded panty hose and old scarves.

He had an assortment of rubber bands, combs, nail clips, packets of Kleenex, safety pins, and cheap handkerchiefs. Things just as useful and necessary to tunnel-dwellers as to anyone else. More important, his "business" gave him a sense of himself. As long as he had his stock and the means to deal he wasn't lost.

"Say Bo," Ralphie Potato yelled out.

"I can hear. You think I'm deaf?" Bo Wango complained, rousing from the doze into which he had fallen.

"You know this fella?" Ralphie asked.

Wango peered up into Seagrave's face.

"Don't know him. Not one of us. Too clean," Bo Wango laughed.

"This man is a writer for the newspaper. He wants to say something nice about old Peg."

"Need any pins, any rubber bands, any Kleenex to wipe yourself?" Bo Wango wheedled.

Seagrave tried two bucks, figuring that this bizarre character would be less in touch with the going rate for favors. Bo Wango grinned, showing several missing teeth, and tucked his hands under his knees. He might trade for pennies, but he wouldn't be interviewed for a couple of bucks. Seagrave sighed and added another three.

Ralphie Potato laughed.

"You sure you guys haven't got a little eight-room duplex over on the Park?" Seagrave complained.

That got Bo Wango to laughing too.

"What do you know about Mumblety Peg?" Seagrave asked.

"She made a good Mulligan," Bo Wango answered, cutting his eyes at Ralphie Potato.

They were playing to each other, having fun with the outsider, the square John, the straight citizen.

"Don't mess me around," Seagrave said harshly. "Why don't you get the hell out of here, Ralphie Potato? You showed me the way."

Ralphie went off without protest, laughing all the way. Seagrave squatted down on his haunches so that he could look at Bo Wango eye to eye.

"How did Peg die?" Seagrave asked.

"Somebody beat her up."

"That all?"

"That's all I know. What else? Was there something else?"

"I was told she got knifed."

"Oh, Jesus," Bo Wango said, and winced as though he could feel the blade slipping into him. "Maud's Sister told me that. She washed old Peg and dressed her up for her funeral."

"How many were at the funeral?"

Bo Wango looked up at the ceiling. His lips moved. He was counting up the mourners.

37.

St. Luke in the Fields Church in the Village is very old as far as things in America are concerned. It goes back to 1822, when the Village was just that and not much bigger than Washington Square. It still retains the feelings of a country church, homely and comforting.

Malloy took a pew halfway down the center aisle. It was so quiet in the cavern of stone that the characters in the stained glass windows seemed to be whispering to one another. There was a big wooden cross on the altar. It seemed odd to Malloy, and then he realized that St. Luke's was Lutheran and their use of the symbol of the cross did not include the poor tortured man nailed to it, as it did in all the Roman Catholic churches of Malloy's boyhood.

This was a house of another faith, but the sounds and

180

smells were much the same. Odor of paper and wood, wax and dust. And the comforting gloom, cool and muted.

He'd been married in church. Not the full production number with cutaways and flowers placed at the foot of the statue of the Virgin. Helen hadn't dared go that far, although she hadn't hesitated to wear white and allow everyone to make the usual jokes about what they both were going to lose on their wedding night.

Malloy had joked about it once, but Helen had frosted him and let him know that matters such as their activities before marriage were not to be joked about, or even mentioned. Her maidenhead and chastity had been regenerated once marriage with Malloy had become a certainty.

Not that it mattered a damn bit. What mattered was the general phoniness that described Helen's life, the phoniness first demonstrated by her wedding dress hypocrisy.

Had he loved her?

There was a phrase to conjure with. Helen had complained that the only thing he loved was his job and his uniform. Irma often said nearly the same thing, in a different way, so perhaps they were right.

Whatever the truth, Malloy simply knew that he preferred the human contacts available to him on a "come as you are" basis down in the tunnels and subway stations. Fierce loyalties hidden behind careless greetings, real concern for friends identified by no more than a casual word and a lifted hand. Help given, never meaning that obligation was implied. Clean and sweet, like a raft appearing out of nowhere when drowning was imminent.

Someone came in the door at Malloy's back. No more than a whisper of footsteps, the slight creak of the old oiled wood as someone seeking comfort, or simple physical ease, sat down.

Malloy turned his head as though examining the stained glass windows over his right shoulder. He could see only the

181

corner of a shoulder behind a pillar when he slanted his eyes.

He reached into his pocket and took out the note, which was as stained and crumpled as the envelope it had come in. He read it again.

"If you want to know about something, come to St. Luke's in the Village, any night this week after dark. You don't come, I'll know you don't want to know."

No signature. No way of knowing who sent the letter to him, if it hadn't been that Eddie B had given it to Tony for delivery in person.

Why couldn't Eddie B have just walked up to Malloy when he was on his rounds? Malloy wasn't all that hard to find.

Malloy thought about Eddie B. He knew his story. What was in the bottle that was so much better than respectability and success? What was lacking in the real world that drove the man Eddie B had once been to go looking for it down in the guts of the city?

He'd had his own flirtation with the slow death at the bottom of the jug. After he'd taken the slugs in his body, and after he'd been pensioned off, it seemed a way to go. For the pain, he'd said. Day after day, sitting in the window of the apartment, watching the street and marking off the hours with a thumbnail on a bottle of rye.

Oddly enough, it hadn't been his drinking that'd become the straw that had broken Helen's back. It had been the sobriety that followed Malloy's understanding that he was playing the fool. Maybe the role of martyr hadn't been too uncomfortable for her particular brand of Catholic conscience, and, besides, martyrs get a lot of attention and sympathy.

When Malloy set out to make amends to her, she'd smiled as sweetly as though her mouth were filled with sugar and forgiven him his transgressions. After a while, when he was back working, industrious and sober, working hard at the role of good husband, all debts paid to her as nearly as they could ever be paid, she'd remind him, gently, off-handedly, of all she'd suffered in the dog days of their marriage.

Finally one day Malloy had said to her, "Helen, you keep on handing me the same bill. I've paid that bill a hundred times. I'm sick and tired of it. I'm not going to keep on playing Mary Magdalene to your Jesus Christ. I want you to stop forgiving me."

That had been close to blasphemy, heresy at the least. Helen had gone home to Mother that night, after picking a quarrel about something else altogether, the television.

Malloy had been alone for a long time after that. It was just the way he'd wanted to be.

Then he'd met Irma one vicious night when he'd brought one of the walking wounded up out of the tunnels into Belle-vue Emergency. She'd been standing there in the middle of some disaster, with blood all over her butcher's apron and the floor, giving orders in language that would have singed the hair of a stevedore with the softest mouth Malloy had seen in a long, long time.

He'd just stood there grinning at her until she'd asked him what the hell he saw that was so goddamn funny.

"My God, you are something," he'd said, and for no reason he, or she for that matter, could ever explain, she'd thrown her arms around him and hugged him.

Malloy laughed out loud. It sounded like a pistol crack, echoing around the walls and empty pews.

"What's funny, Malloy?" a voice whispered at his back.

His appointment had arrived as promised, but Malloy knew it wasn't Eddie B.

38.

With a conviction that left no doubt about the accuracy of his memory, Bo Wango named off all eighteen mourners in Mumblety Peg's funeral cortege.

"You know every one of them?" Seagrave asked.

"Except the last two," Bo Wango said. "Except for the one called Phiz and the one called Jay-Jay. They was casuals."

"Were they cleared in the tunnels?"

"Oh, yes. They knew the high signs and the go-aheads, but they was new. I could tell."

"How come they were in on the ceremony?"

Bo Wango thought about that for a minute.

"They know Peg?" Seagrave urged.

"I don't think so. I think they come with Reverend Moss. I think they was under his wing."

Seagrave nodded. The Reverend Moss was no minister, but he did more for the spiritual and physical well-being of the tunnel-dwellers than any of the authorities and churches topside could ever hope to do, even if they had the will to try.

"Mumblety Peg have any best friends?" the reporter asked next.

"Me, I think. Maud's Sister was the closest, maybe. Next to Linus Bean, that is. He played games with her all the time after she gave him supper."

That one almost slipped by. Seagrave was so intent on the questioning, trying to sort out eighteen losers, most of whom he knew, but not that well, that the mention of games, the very thing he'd based a running story on, nearly got away.

"Anybody else?" he asked.

"Eddie B. Eddie B knows just about everybody though, so I don't know if he's anybody's friend."

Then it hit. Seagrave finally heard the answer, last but one.

"Games?"

"Eddie B don't play games," Bo Wango said.

"This Linus."

"Yeah, I just said. Played games with old Peg. Liked to devil her sometimes."

"How do you mean?"

"Well, she told me once she suspected he was stealing pieces of one of her games because he didn't much like to play that one with her."

"Which game?"

"Monopoly," Bo Wango said.

"Ahh," Seagrave breathed. He felt his instincts, his nose for news, had just delivered a jackpot into his hands.

"Do I know this Linus?" he asked.

"How the hell should I know?" Bo Wango asked.

"I mean, where might I have seen him?"

"Works the schoolboy beggar dodge," Bo Wango said.

"Whereabouts?"

"Here and there," Bo Wango replied in the motto of the wanderers.

"What does he look like?"

Bo Wango described Linus fairly well. It sounded like a thousand kids but Seagrave just knew it was the kid he snapped at the disaster. The hero.

"Eddie B would probably know where he is," Bo Wango volunteered.

"They friends?"

"Used to be. Eddie B doesn't like him any more, I don't think."

"So why would he know where Linus is then?"

"Any fool knows a man keeps closer tabs on his enemies than his friends."

"Where can I find Eddie B?"

"What time is it?"

Seagrave glanced at his watch and told Bo Wango the hour.

"Eddie B will be sleeping."

"Where?"

"What day is it?"

"Wednesday," Seagrave said sharply. Bo Wango was getting on his nerves.

"He's in the tunnel, in a hole, underneath the Waldorf."

"He has a nice address," Seagrave joked sardonically.

"He does his best," Bo Wango said and looked at Seagrave with eyes that were not too foolish.

Eddie B was in the niche in the wall underneath the Waldorf-Astoria just as promised, sleeping on a pile of old rags and newspapers. When Seagrave stooped down and jostled him very easily, Eddie B woke up with the defensive start common to drunks and vagrants, throwing up his hands in front of his face and drawing up his knees to protect his most sensitive parts.

186

"Don't hit me," he screamed thinly. "I ain't got nothing."

Seagrave moved back a pace or two, still squatting down so that he wouldn't loom over the frightened man and seem more formidable.

"I'm not here to hurt you, Eddie B," Seagrave said soothingly.

Eddie B squinted up at him. He wiped his mouth with the back of his hand. It seemed to force a smell of cheap wine into the air, as though the move had squeezed it out of his pores.

"I know you?" Eddie B asked.

"No."

"You know me?"

"Well, I know about you," Seagrave said.

"What's that mean?"

"I asked Bo Wango where you were."

"What for?"

"I wanted to talk to you."

"What about?"

Seagrave didn't answer, but cocked his head as though listening for something.

"What's the matter?" Eddie B asked.

"You hear anything?" Seagrave asked in return.

Eddie B listened carefully, his eyes growing wide with the effort.

"Who do you think might be trying to walk so soft?" Seagrave said.

"I don't hear anything," Eddie B whispered.

"Could it be that son of a bitch Linus?"

"You know Linus?"

"I'm looking for Linus, yes," Seagrave said. "You know where he is?"

Eddie B's eyes grew narrow with suspicion.

"Why do you want to find him?"

"Well, not to do him any favors."

"Ain't you his friend?"

187

"Not likely."

"What then?"

Seagrave shuffled in closer. "I can only tell you that when I find him I don't intend to hand him a fiver like I intend giving you."

"Intend?" Eddie B said, testing the meaning of the word.

A little awkwardly, Seagrave snagged five bucks from the pocket of his pants and folded it double, creasing the green along its length in front of Eddie B's wondering eyes.

"If you know where Linus is," Seagrave cooed.

"I'm not certain, mind."

"I can't expect guarantees," Seagrave agreed.

Never taking his eyes off the bill, Eddie B told the reporter that he suspected Linus was at St. Luke's in Greenwich Village.

"How do you know that?" Seagrave asked.

"I can't swear to it. I don't know for sure. But he'll be there sooner or later this week."

"All right. But how do you know it?"

"Because I asked Malloy to meet me there, and Linus got that news out of me," Eddie B nearly shouted, as though he were scared or angry.

Seagrave hurried up into the open air, flagged a cab, and gave the address of the church on Hudson Street.

188

39.

"Don't turn around, Malloy," Linus said.

Malloy straightened up a bit.

"Don't!" Linus warned again.

Malloy had an idea, but he asked anyway.

"Who is it?"

"Who were you expecting?"

Malloy was silent, mulling that one over. He didn't want to put Eddie B in jeopardy.

"You were expecting Eddie B, weren't you?" Linus said.

"Why didn't he come?" Malloy asked.

Linus giggled softly. "I came instead."

Malloy wondered if Eddie B was dead as well, having angered the sick kid who sat at his back.

"Is Eddie B sick?"

"No."

"Is he . . ." Malloy started to say.

Linus jumped right on the sentence. ". . . dead? No, he isn't dead. What makes you think that?"

"I didn't say I thought he was dead. I just asked."

"You think I go around killing the people I know just like that?"

"You killed one."

"Oh, Jesus," Linus moaned. There was a strangled sound to his voice as though tears were flooding his throat.

"You killed Mumblety Peg, didn't you?"

"Shut up," Linus whispered fiercely.

"You killed Mary Finney," Malloy said.

"Who?" Linus exclaimed as though his mind had wandered off and he'd missed a beat.

"Mary Finney. The girl on the Coney Island Express."

There was silence at Malloy's back. He leaned over and placed the palms of his hands in the wells of his eyes.

"What's the matter?" Linus said.

"I've got a headache."

"I know what that's like. Jesus, don't I know what that's like," Linus said emphatically.

"That was you killed Mary Finney, wasn't it?"

"She yelled. She acted like I was going to hurt her. I wasn't going to hurt her. I just wanted to tell her a funny thing."

"What funny thing?"

"I was going to tell her there was another girl got off at the Brooklyn Museum station dressed just like her."

"Is that all you wanted to say?"

"Swear to God. But she started yelling."

"Oh, my," Malloy breathed to himself and felt like crying. "Why did you knife Mr. Morrison?"

"Which one was he? I'm not good remembering names."

"The man wearing the homburg hat."

"Businessman. Looked like a businessman."

190

"That's what he was. Somebody's husband, too. Somebody's father."

"What are you trying to do, Malloy, break my back? You trying to make me feel guilty for stabbing that geek?"

"I'm trying to understand why you did it."

"Who said I did anything?" Linus protested. "Is that what I said? Is that what I said?"

Malloy sat motionless. The killer behind him was swinging like a pendulum.

"You know who killed the woman in the theater party? Mrs. Spector?" Malloy went on.

"Maybe."

"Why would anybody want to kill a nice little woman like that?"

"She was making like she cared. She was worrying about Bean getting cold."

"Is that why he killed her? Did Bean kill her because she was kind?"

"Can't trust that sort of thing."

"Crazy."

"Maybe you're right."

Linus sighed. The sigh was deep and tragic, and trembled at the end.

"Oh, God, I killed them all. You think I'm crazy?"

"Could be."

"Yeah, I think maybe I am. You know anyone can tell me what's crazy? How can you tell a crazy?"

Malloy thought of Mercado, his white hair, and nervous hands, his kind eyes and how he always said there wasn't a scratch to peek through yet on the black glass that concealed the workings of the mind.

"I know somebody who could at least talk to you about what's bothering you."

"Who said anything's bothering me?"

"Hey, let it go. You don't have to play games any more."

191

"Yeah, games. Peg always wanted to play games. Liked games."

"You like games?"

"Oh, yeah." Linus was silent for a while.

Honker sat behind the pillar, smelling the alien odors of alien worship, and wondered what the hell was going on now. Malloy was looking down at his hands or nodding off. Linus was sitting hunched over, his hands in the pockets of his trousers. Hair falling in his eyes. Silent as a mouse now. Not whispering or half shouting. Not laughing or grunting angrily.

Honker had almost made a move a half a dozen times. Waiting was hard. He wanted to move, but was afraid he'd blow the collar somehow.

"You know something about games?" Linus asked, breaking the silence.

"What?"

"The thing I don't like about games?"

"What's that?"

"Well, after the game's over. If you win it, it doesn't mean all that much. Somebody just lays out the pieces again and you have to start all over."

"Yeah, yeah, yeah," Malloy said softly, which was like saying "Amen."

"And sometimes it's even worse. Sometimes somebody changes the rules right in the middle of the game. Or maybe they don't explain them good enough at the start."

"Yeah," Malloy breathed.

"Never any rest. Game starts up all over again," Linus raved on, his voice getting stringy and high.

"Why don't you get some rest?" Malloy asked.

"Oh, Christ, I'd like that."

192

"A little peace and quiet. You want a little peace and quiet inside your head, don't you?"

"You talking about dead? I don't want to be dead."

"Neither do I."

"They'll kill me if they get me."

"Who?"

"They will."

"Ah, no. They'll help you. They'll know it wasn't your fault."

Malloy felt sad. He wanted to believe what he was saying, that they'd help him, but what one person means by help isn't the same thing at all that somebody else means.

Malloy turned around to look, and Linus didn't protest.

"Sure," Malloy said. It served to mean a lot. It meant that he wanted Linus to know that he, at least, knew it wasn't Linus's fault. Not in any way that can be measured or judged, though perhaps in ways that might be punished or isolated. It meant that Malloy was softly chiding himself for wondering about the young fellow seemingly waiting for one train too many at the scene of the Puerto Rican's death, and then forgetting about the suspicion after the explosion. Then there was the fact that Malloy had seen the kid playing the student dodge a hundred times, but never made the connection.

"Sure," he said. "Nobody'll hurt you."

"Like hell," Linus hissed. "They'll take me into a cell down in the basement and beat the crap out of me. They'll punch me in the throat and punish my kidneys with pieces of hose. They'll pound my belly with wet towels and bust up my guts."

"No, no," Malloy said soothingly.

There were tears running down Linus's cheeks. He swiped them away with one hand.

"Don't look at me," he ordered. "Turn around."

Malloy did as he was told. He didn't want Linus running off.

193

"They won't do anything like that if I take you in. I'll let everybody know that I brought you in without a mark. I'll tell them that if they hurt you—lay so much as a finger on you—I'll blow the whistle on them."

He waited to see what response that would bring.

Finally he added wearily, as though he had no other offers to make, "They know me. They know I'll do what I say. I keep my word."

"That's what they say in the tunnels," Linus agreed. "That's what they say."

"How you want to work this? Want to come with me now?" Malloy asked.

"I guess there's no reason why not. Move over a little. I want to give you something."

Malloy shifted over in his seat.

Honker saw the kid take his hand out of his pocket. He saw the flash of a knife blade. He saw Linus slide out of the pew and move into the one where Malloy sat.

He didn't see Linus close the blade against his hip, ready to turn the murder weapon over to the man he was allowing to be his captor.

Honker was on his feet and running, shouting at the top of his lungs.

Malloy and Linus turned to the rattling cry at the same moment.

"You lousy, rotten son of a bitch," Linus cried out in rage. He flicked open the knife and swiped at Malloy's head. Malloy turned around to say that he didn't know Honker Levine had been lurking in the shadows of the church. The blade cut a path across his neck. Linus ran down the aisle.

Honker passed through the row of seats, pulling at the police special tucked into his belt.

Malloy, one hand grabbing his neck where the blood welled, stepped in front of Honker.

"Don't shoot, for Christ's sake!" he yelled.

Honker saw that Linus had disappeared through a side

door out to the street. Cold air came sweeping into the church. Candles on the altar guttered fitfully.

They held each other in a kind of embrace looking into each other's eyes.

"For Christ's sake," Malloy said.

Out on the street Seagrave was just pulling up in the cab. He saw the fleeing Linus. He recognized him as the young man who'd played the hero in the subway disaster, the one whose picture he'd taken and put on the front page.

40.

After the recriminations and angry accusations of hotdog-
ging were done, after Gertie had called him a grandstanding
son of a bitch gimpy ex-cop trying to relive and repair an
old mistake, Malloy was left alone with Mercado.

"You spoke with him, then?" Mercado said softly.

"Yeah."

"What can you tell me?"

"What do you mean?" Malloy asked leaning forward a
little from his seat in the corner.

"What made him kill? Did he say?"

"He didn't have reasons if that's what you mean. Just . . ."

"Yes?"

"Just headaches. Just frustrations."

"Is that what he said?"

"Not exactly."

196

"I wish you'd tell me what he said. As much as you can remember. I'd like to know," Mercado asked, making it a humble request.

Malloy told him then what Linus had said about games and the way they were never over even if you won, but the pieces were just laid out again and the game had to start all over.

Mercado simply nodded his head as though Malloy had told him the answer to some deep dark secret.

"Are you all right, Malloy?" he asked.

"What?" Malloy responded vaguely.

Mercado pointed to the bloody handkerchief and the tie that kept it tight against the wound.

"You want me to look at that? I'm a doctor, you know. I once did it for a living."

Malloy stood up.

"No, no. I think I'll go on over to Bellevue. Let Irma take care of it."

"She'd like that," Mercado said as though Malloy intended to give his woman a gift.

Malloy walked to the door. He nearly stumbled a little at a worn spot in the tile, but he recovered himself and Mercado didn't make a move to help.

Seagrave called to Malloy from the cab waiting at the curb.

Malloy went over.

"I saw the kid run out of the church. His name is Linus Bean."

"Ahh," Malloy nodded.

"He was the one who helped you save that woman's life, you know?"

"Yeah. Now ain't that a hell of a story?" Malloy smiled, and Seagrave knew they were friends again.

"Going somewhere?" he asked.

197

"To see a nurse."

"Taking the subway?"

"I thought I would."

"Well, get in. Let me give you a taste of the easy life."

Malloy almost refused the ride but thought Seagrave might take it as a slight. Patching up damaged friendships was a touchy business. He got inside and immediately felt the closeness and the heat, worse in its way than anything the trains had to offer except at the height of the rush hour.

"Can you tell me what happened?" Seagrave asked.

"That the price of the ride?" Malloy said flatly.

"Hell, no. We won't argue about newspaper ethics right now, but you'll have to admit a little coverage might help find this character now that you know who he is. At least credit me with an assist. Accident or no, I got a picture of him."

"It helped. Or it could have helped if things had gone down differently. One of the friends of Mrs. Spector called me on it. She recognized him."

"Then I'm entitled to a little something?"

"As much as anybody else, I suppose," Malloy said and told Seagrave most of the conversation that had passed between Linus and himself.

"Doesn't tell us much about him, does it?"

"Sort of like an obit. That doesn't tell much about a man either."

"Unless he's famous."

"Maybe not even then. All you can really know about a famous person is the way they wore their face."

Seagrave started to get out at Bellevue, meaning to help Malloy, but Malloy waved him back.

"Go write a story," he said.

"It could do some good, you know?" Seagrave offered. "Yeah?"

"When I write that this kid Linus Bean is suspected of the

198

knifing death of old Mumblety Peg, he might find some of his hiding places closed to him."

"He's used to that," Malloy said. He waved a hand like a salute and shut the door of the cab, then turned away to go into Emergency.

Irma rushed across the floor toward him, her face paler than usual. He could tell somebody had already told her about what had happened, at least that he'd been hurt.

"Get over here, get over here," she said.

Malloy stumbled then and she was quick to get underneath his arm and hold him up. As Godowski moved to help she shook her head fiercely and then gave him the high sign to lose himself.

She sat Malloy down on a gurney in one of the examination cubicles.

"How come it's so quiet?" Malloy said.

Irma shrugged her shoulders and wiped her hands down the front of her stainless apron.

"I was hoping people were getting good with one another," she said.

She untied the knot on the tie that held the makeshift bandage in place, and then examined it.

"What is it?" Malloy said.

"Looking for blood stains."

"What a thing to say."

"Cost me twenty bucks last Christmas."

"I mean, Jesus, Irma, here I am wounded," Malloy grinned, "wounded in the line of duty, and you're checking my tie for damage."

She kissed him on the cheek and took the wadded handkerchief from his neck. It pulled a little and he winced.

"Doesn't need any sewing," Irma said. "How the hell did you let him get close enough to let him do this?"

"He was just slipping into the pew beside me. He wasn't intending to use it."

"How the hell could you know that?"

"He wanted a place to rest. He wanted a place where he wouldn't be hurt. I told him I'd get it for him. He trusted me."

"So you had to trust him?"

"The knife was closed when he started to sit down. I heard the blade flip out when Honker yelled and spooked him."

"You telling me a goddamn cop set you up for this?"

"Didn't set me up. He thought I was in trouble."

"This the same cop that's been making like your shadow?"

Malloy nodded.

"Well, Christ, didn't you know he might go after the killer?"

"I thought Honker was home with a cold," Malloy said sheepishly. Irma swabbed out the cut with disinfectant and Malloy winced again.

"Ouch, Irma," he said.

"Don't faint, tough guy. You should have come right in here before reporting in to Posner." She applied a bandage.

"There was still a chance we could have picked him up before he went to ground," Malloy said.

Malloy slid off the gurney. He tottered a little. Irma caught him around the waist and he grinned down into her face.

"You know, wise guy," Irma said very softly, "another half inch and he'd have nicked the jugular."

"Maybe now I'll faint."

He kissed her.

"You and me both," she joked.

"Everybody tells me nurses are tough."

"What else they tell you?"

"Nurses are easy."

"The hell you say."

"You know. Being around all that dirt and pain. Makes them grateful for a little tender loving care."

"Know anybody who's got any?"

Malloy looked over her shoulder and reached out to part

200

the curtains a little so that he could see into the reception area. He pushed against Irma.

"What the hell's that?" she yelped softly.

"Awful goddamn quiet around here," he said.

"It happens. Now back off, Malloy. You're a horny Irishman."

He took another step, pressing himself against her pelvis. She stepped back one.

"You're filthy," she said.

"Hey!"

"Your clothes. Your clothes are filthy. Besides I don't make love against a wall . . ."

Malloy reached back and patted the gurney.

"Don't need a wall," he said.

". . . against a wall with a big stupid subway cop with a lousy haircut and a bloody shirt," she went on, her hands against his chest.

"All right. I'll go home and make myself pretty. Pick you up at the end of shift."

"Maybe you shouldn't," Irma frowned. "You might be weaker than you think."

"Hey," Malloy said. "I don't see you tonight I could go a little crazy."

"We got a good thing, Malloy. We're both a little crazy," Irma said.

41.

The citizens of the tunnel were the failed and the castoff, the misfits, losers, has-beens, and those who'd never been at all. Even an exploiter and enforcer like Ralphie Potato was a fraud, able to be cock-o-the-walk only in a world of such weakness that even a threatening gesture was enough to establish supremacy.

When the suspicions that Eddie B had harbored spread among Mumblety Peg's friends and acquaintances—Maud's Sister, Harry the Hangnail, Bo Wango, Benny the Fool, the Reverend Moss, and the rest—and from their mouths to the ears of all who lived in the tunnels, there was much whispered talk about what they should do about the killer among them.

It was suggested that he be banished, thrown into exile to the world above. Made to risk the streets and the fatal alleys. Ralphie Potato loudly proclaimed that a group of enforcers should punish Linus unmercifully so that he would never have the foolish daring to raise his hand against one of them. The Reverend Moss spoke of "a nation of laws" no different from the one that existed in the straight world. It was his thought that they should bring Linus to trial, making sure that they were not condemning him on the evidence offered by that other world.

All careless surmise, silly chatter, brave posturings. They would do nothing, not even Ralphie Potato and his bully boys. At least not now, when the news was fresh on their tongues.

But, later, Linus thought, some hero among them or a group made bold with bottles of cheap muscatel might decide to execute him for the sake of their pride.

He made a section of a tunnel his own, huddling in a service niche so that he would always be facing any attack. He slept sitting up with his back against the wall, his legs drawn up, arms wrapped around them, resting his head on his knees. His knife was always open, lying close to hand, whenever he rested. It seemed a puny weapon.

He went out to get a gun.

In the night he journeyed up and out into the air. He broke into a hardware store way out at the end of the line in Astoria and stole nothing more than a powerful set of bolt cutters. Back in the heart of the city, he cut the screen guarding the window of a pawn shop, its windows filled with goods given over by the desperate and destitute. He smashed the window and stole the first handgun that was available, a thirty-two Special, and a box of ammunition to suit.

The alarm screamed out fit to wake the dead. Not a window in the tenements surrounding was opened. Not a light in any unlit window came on.

"The great danger is this," Mercado said, offering another of his scenarios. "Linus may really feel betrayed now. He

203

went to the church prepared to give himself up . . ."

"We don't know that," Posner interrupted. "That's how it looked like it was going down at the end, but that was only after Malloy had talked to him. Made promises."

"Agreed," Mercado nodded. "I accept the amendment. Perhaps he had gone to St. Luke's to do still another person harm. "This time an officer, a symbol of authority. But something in Malloy's sympathy for the boy urged him to give it up."

"Until that sheenie uniform decided to play hero," Gertie said.

"Ah, ah, ah," Posner warned, waving his hand with the palm toward Gertie. "If Levine made the collar you'd be sitting there telling us what a shrewd judge of men you are. Maybe what Levine did was bad luck, but it wasn't bad judgment. He saw the glint of a blade, Malloy's back was turned, and Honker acted on it."

Posner looked at Malloy toward the end of his statement. Malloy nodded, giving his blessing to what the lieutenant had said.

"So enough," Posner finished. He looked at Mercado again.

"There's no telling what Linus might do now. A knife might not be quick enough, bad enough. One on one might not satisfy him any more. He could be ready to go out of control, figuring he has nowhere to turn and nothing to lose. He might get his hands on some guns or explosives."

Mercado shrugged helplessly.

"There's no telling," he finished.

Ralphie Potato, Eddie B, Bo Wango, and the others might not have been brave enough to throw Linus out of their city bodily, but they were ingenious and inventive.

They devised a plan of harassment. They endeavored to make certain that Linus was never given much of a chance

204

to sleep. When they found him curled up in his tunnel they set up a terrible din with pots and pans scavenged from garbage cans. Eddie B found a battered trumpet and blew blasting notes from a place as near as he dared get to Linus's den. When Linus was driven from his territory to seek tunnels farther out, there were guerrillas there as well, leaving him no place to hide.

One day Bo Wango got too near, in a place without concealment. Linus fired at him, and one of the bullets struck his leg. After that they were more careful, but their attacks upon Linus increased in magnitude and fury. He was an animal gone mad, a danger to everyone.

Finally he was driven out of the steam tunnels, and every quiet corner. The only place he could find any relief from their constant oppression was in the subway stations.

In these no man's lands Linus held on to the gun hidden beneath his sweater and plotted the nature of his revenge.

42.

It was raining so hard that it seemed nature intended to prove this was to be the last rain of spring. It flooded the gutters and the sewers. Streets were streams and avenues rivers. Some of the overload even swamped the tunnels and ran along the roadbeds in places. It served to keep practically everyone off the streets at six o'clock at night.

Except Malloy. He went down to check on Irma at Bellevue as though he'd finally learned that there was another world besides the one under the concrete, but he wasn't yet ready to take the straight world at one swallow. Bellevue was like a halfway house.

It was another of the rare, quiet shifts.

"The weather," Irma said. "Sometimes a rain like this brings emergencies, sometimes a kind of . . ."

When she hesitated for the word, Malloy said, ". . . peace?"

206

She laughed with a touch of embarrassment as though such considerations were grossly sentimental.

"Where's the doctors?" he asked.

"Getting all the sleep they can steal," Irma smiled. Malloy looked over his shoulder to the place where Godowski sat, arms folded on his chest, nodding off.

"He a good conversationalist?" Malloy smiled.

"Sometimes. If you like to talk about sports, hookers, and brands of beer."

"The simple life," Malloy said.

Irma tapped her pencil on the form she was filling out.

"There's not much chance for conversation around here even when it's quiet," she said. "Paper work. There's never a shortage of it."

Malloy tilted his head as though trying to read what was on the paper.

"Report on fractures. Last year's. Surveys make the world go 'round."

"If we can count 'em, maybe we can do something about 'em?"

A nurse popped her head around the corner of the hallway.

"Still okay, Irma?" she asked.

"Still okay," Irma said and the nurse went off again.

Malloy raised his eyebrows.

"She stealing some sleep too?" he asked.

Irma grinned. "No, but I think she's about to use a bed."

Lightning crashed outside. Several moments later thunder rumbled down the streets and shook the windowpanes.

"Across the river," Malloy said.

"You look tired, Malloy."

"Yeah."

"You should be home. You should know enough to stay out of the rain."

"Yeah."

"You're not still hunting the subways for that boy?"

207

"He might show himself. After all, it's the only home he's got."

"Well, it's not the only one you've got. Go home and put your feet up, Malloy."

He still hesitated, seeming reluctant to lose contact with her.

"Something?" she asked.

"I guess not."

There was something. Bad feelings all over his body. Not physical unease, but something else. Anxiety. Apprehension. A certain disquiet, both chronic and acute. He didn't want to burden Irma with his insubstantial fears and misgivings.

"Hey," she said, reaching out to place her hand on his. "Why don't I come over to your place after my shift?"

"On Wednesday?"

"What are we, old stick-in-the-muds? Have our brains gone stiff? Can't we break a habit?"

Malloy brightened up.

"All right," he said enthusiastically. "I'll wait for you. I'll just sit over there and wait for you."

"No, no, no. Go back to your place. Do something romantic."

He stared at her as though he hadn't a thought in his head.

"Light some candles. Spray some perfume around the joint." She laughed.

"Perfume?"

"So use aftershave. Chill a couple bottles of wine. Buy some smoked salmon and caviar. Seduce me."

Malloy leaned over the charge desk to kiss Irma. His eyes were happy for the moment. He was like a child who had been offered a gorgeous new game to play. He was also grabbing at straws to keep back his premonition of disaster.

He tapped Godowski on the way out. The big, good-natured orderly jerked his head up and grinned.

"Was I sleeping?" he asked.

"That's what it looked like to me," Malloy answered him

as he swept out of the emergency exit into the rain, which was now lessening somewhat.

Godowski looked over at Irma and their eyes met.

"I wasn't sleeping, Irma," he said.

"I know," she smiled. "You're just a tactful romantic."

"I am, I am," Godowski said and got up to stretch.

He poked around in his pockets and came up with part of a pack of cigarettes. He fished one out and straightened it out, pleased that the paper wasn't broken. He fumbled around a little more and came up with a book of matches, lit the cigarette, and then, after a puff or two, went out to smell the air in the dying rain.

Malloy was at the curb, waiting for the light, even though there wasn't a car in sight. Godowski huddled in the doorway. The rain was no more than a drizzle, but it was still chilly, the wind keen when it blew.

Irma went back to the form. She checked the statistics with the card file, wondered what would happen to all the figures she wrote down. Did anyone even read them?

A shiver caught her in the small of the back and ran up to her shoulder blades. The old saying about "somebody walking on my grave" popped into her mind. She lifted her head, listening. She couldn't remember the hospital ever being so quiet. After a long moment of concentration she could begin to hear the distant sounds of activity. A dish rattling somewhere far off. A cough. The opening of a door down the corridor.

Linus opened the door into the hallway. He had come up through the many basements. He carried the gun. It was loaded. He carried the knife as well. The first death he intended to cause this night would be done with a knife.

More personal that way, he thought, and smiled softly to himself. He crept along the floor on rubber-soled tennis shoes. At the door into the Emergency area he paused and looked carefully through the window set in it.

He saw only one person. There was a nurse sitting at the charge desk writing. She lifted her head. It was Malloy's girlfriend, the one Linus had come to destroy. Punishment for the man who had lied to him.

Irma lowered her head again. She forced herself to give every bit of her attention to the forms. Best to get it over with. She didn't hear his footsteps behind he

Malloy was halfway down the block on his way to the subway station when he thought of something he wanted to ask Irma before he went to the late hour deli for the food he was expected to provide. He turned around and walked back to the light. It was red against him and again he waited. This time a few cars were passing on the street.

Godowski was puffing on his cigarette, telling himself there were three things he was going to do very soon. One, stop smoking. Two, cool it on the beer. Three, lose some weight. He took another long drag, enjoying it immensely, since he'd soon be deprived of the cutting sensation.

Linus touched the button on the knife. He did it deliberately close to Irma's ear, hand outstretched so that she would be sure to hear it. She whirled around in a flash, then immediately stood up, her mind racing, forcing herself to remember what she'd learned as a student nurse on the psycho ward.

"Didn't I tell you to wait?" she said in a scolding voice.

"What are you talking about?" Linus said, startled and confused.

"I told you to wait. I'm sure I told you to wait. So many people hurt."

Linus glanced around the quiet, empty space in some confusion. What was she talking about? Then he understood.

210

"That was a long time ago," he complained. "I came to you a long time ago."

"I know, and I told you to sit down and wait," Irma insisted again.

"You didn't pay any attention to me."

"Don't be silly."

"Watch yourself," Linus warned.

"I mean you misunderstood what was happening. I wasn't shoving you off to the side. You looked like you were able to wait. That girl . . ."

"I know," Linus interrupted.

"What do you know?"

"I saw her face."

"Then can't you see I had to help her first?"

"I was hurt," Linus hissed angrily.

"That girl might have died."

"Then let her die."

"You don't mean that."

"Let everybody die," Linus said, and smiled.

Malloy reached the hospital side of the street.

"Forget something?" Godowski asked.

"Irma said something about wanting caviar."

"Expensive tastes," the orderly grinned.

"Champagne goes with caviar."

"I never drink nothing else with mine," Godowski said.

"Irma doesn't even like champagne."

"Then don't get any."

"I don't think she much likes caviar either."

"Then don't get any of that either."

"Yeah, but she told me to get something special. You know?"

It was a curious puzzle. Godowski was giving it everything he had. He understood the sensitivity of the decision. When a lady said she wanted something special it usually had some romantic or sentimental meaning hidden behind it. Either that or . . .

"Hey! Irma's not . . ."

Malloy grinned.

"No. She's not pregnant."

Laughing, he started toward the Emergency entrance. Then he stopped laughing and walking at the same moment. Could that be the matter? Could that be the reason for her appetite for things she usually disliked?

"You want me to look at that wound in your side?" Irma asked.

"How do you know where I was cut?"

"Can't you believe that I remember things about you? Can't you believe that I wasn't shining you off?"

"Okay."

"Well, let me have a look at how it's healing."

She took a step toward Linus. He backed up.

"What are you trying to do?"

"Trying to help you."

"That's what your boyfriend said he was going to do."

Irma gasped.

"That's right. I'm the guy in the church. I guess he told you. I'm 'the Monopoly Killer.' "

When Irma made no response Linus said, "What do you think of that?"

"What am I supposed to think?"

"I know what you're thinking."

"Do you?"

"You're thinking if you keep me talking long enough something will happen, or somebody will walk in. You better hope not."

"May I sit down?" Irma asked.

"You'd better hope not, because if anyone comes in here I'm going to stop talking."

"May I sit down?" Irma asked again without any change in her tone of voice.

"What's the matter?"

"I don't feel well."

"All right. You can sit down."

Irma pulled the old wooden swivel-back chair toward her as though she were too weak or sick to make the three steps it would need to get herself to it. She held on to the back, her eyes on Linus's face. She was ready to swing it around as protection and start screaming when Linus looked over her shoulder.

Malloy came swinging through the doors from outside. He reacted to the situation without a second thought. As he raced toward the counter Irma swept the chair around on its screeching wheels just as Linus made a lunge toward her. The chair seat clipped him on the shins, just below his knee-caps. He let out a howl and stumbled to the side.

Malloy made a dive for the counter, going over it on his belly, reaching out to grab hold of Linus.

Linus wrenched himself away, turned, and started to run as Malloy sprawled half on, half off the charge desk. Malloy tried to push himself upright, using the chair for leverage, but it rolled away from him and he felt himself falling to the floor.

Godowski came running in.

Irma was screaming, not in fear, but in rage. Hospital personnel came racing down the corridors leading to the Emergency Admissions. Linus had already disappeared through the door that opened to the stairway leading down into the basements.

When Malloy got there, he paused, holding on to the metal rail, listening for Linus's steps as they echoed on the metal treads. He was going down. Down. Why not? It was in his nature to go underground. It would be the natural place for him to hide or to make a last stand.

213

43.

There was a bullet of pain between his eyes. Linus struck himself, hoping to drive it away. It didn't do a bit of good. There was another pain where he'd been wounded in the fight with the old Chinese man, and still another in the pit of his stomach. He slammed down the stairways, grabbing the rail and swinging himself around each time he reached a lower landing.

Malloy felt pain as well. The old bullet scars felt like fire and there was a flaming ache beginning deep in the tissues of his hip and belly. He had to take it a little easier. Pace himself. Never let the kid get too far ahead, but don't try to catch up right off. Let Linus panic and race his motor. Let him suck air and burn himself out. Malloy settled into a rhythm, letting the weight of his legs carry him down the steps almost as though he were in a controlled fall.

In the lowest basement Linus thought about hiding. Getting back in among the welter of pipes and boilers and discarded furniture. But instinct feared unknown places. He had his own dens and lairs in the tunnels. He ducked through the green door. He was in the maze of Con Edison tunnels.

He turned back to the door and slammed the handle down into its bracket, then kicked at it until it was bent enough to jam.

Malloy was too late to prevent it. He grasped the handle on his side in both hands and wrenched at it with all his strength. The handle was jammed in tight. Linus was walking off on the other side of it.

Malloy hesitated for a moment, figuring what Linus would do. When a hunted animal goes to ground it heads for a familiar place. But some animals were cunning enough to have half a dozen lairs, and Malloy figured Linus was just such a crafty creature.

He hurried off into the depths of the sub-basement. The air felt cold and dead. There were abandoned and discarded pieces of medical equipment huddled in the shadows. Old beds of experiment and failure and pain. They seemed to be whispering at his back as he passed them.

The secondary access door was back behind a stand of boilers long since taken out of service. A little door not much taller than a two-year-old. Thumbscrews secured the bolts in their clips. They were rusted tight. Malloy found a bar of iron amid the rubble and attacked the toggles with patient, stunning blows. The threads broke and gave way, scattering their rust onto the floor. He opened the door and started through, eeling his way, a joint and a shoulder at a time, smiling all the way. He figured he knew the country at least as well as Linus. He'd been traveling it just that much longer.

*　*　*

215

Linus was no longer in a hurry. It had been too easy, too goddamn easy, he thought. Malloy was nothing. He knew the story of his fall. No wonder he took four bullets in the belly. Dumb bastard.

He passed a service door. He knew it ended in a dead end at a manhole, sealed and forgotten, twenty yards away. He didn't know that Malloy had already broken through from the other end and had his hands right on the door at the moment.

The third barrier gave way easily enough. Malloy came out of the shunt into the main artery. There was the sound of footsteps up ahead. Linus. He wasn't trying to walk cautiously. He thought himself already well free of his pursuer. Malloy got up on the balls of his feet. He ran along, his soles whispering along the concrete. He slowed down when he saw the shape of a man walking in front of him, a darker shape against the growing light at the end of the tunnel.

A train came roaring into the station down there. Malloy couldn't see it, but waves of dusty, frigid air, laced with threads of steam heat, came piling back at him. Linus stopped and half turned away to protect his eyes from the flying dust. His sight was always tuned to the shadows. He saw Malloy, the shadow in the shadows. He started to run. Malloy ran after him.

There were work lamps in wire cages all along the way for this stretch of tunnel. It cast Linus's shadow out before him, elongating it as the angles changed. It threw Malloy's shadow right after it. Sometimes his shadow almost touched Linus, but never caught up to the dark, insubstantial ghost that led the chase.

Linus burst out of the tunnel. He fled along the ledge, behind the slender safety rails, which ran the length of the subway tunnel, toward the station at 28th on the Lexington line.

A train pulled in to the station. Linus stepped aboard. He looked back and saw Malloy step into the next to last car. He counted to four, then stepped out onto the platform. Malloy was watching and stepped out at well. Their eyes were wired together. Linus grinned and stepped back into the car. Malloy did the same. Linus began to laugh. He remembered seeing just what they were doing in some film a couple of years ago. He stepped out again, and quickly drew back when he saw Malloy was sticking with him. The last time he played the game he waited until the doors hissed, ready to close. He jumped through the closing sides. Malloy did the same.

Linus sat down, still laughing. People looked at him out of the corners of their eyes. When he looked at any one of them, that one would quickly look away. He glanced down toward the door at the end of the car, waiting for Malloy to show himself.

The conductor called out the next two stations. He was scarcely intelligible over the bad sound system. "Thirty-third Street. Grand Central."

The train sped on toward the next station. Still Malloy didn't show himself. They were in and out of Thirty-third and he was still nowhere to be seen. Linus got up and walked down to the end of the car. He peered through into the next one. Malloy wasn't there.

"Grand Central Station!" the conductor roared out.

Linus stepped out onto the platform. He looked back toward the end of the train. He tried to spot Malloy but wasn't able to. He began to feel frightened. It was just a razor blade of anxiety cutting into his complacency.

Linus bolted a few steps like a scared pony, then stopped and even took two steps back toward Malloy and a woman with two shopping bags. Malloy approached him, moving people aside with his hands, apologizing as he moved closer to the young man who was shuffling along sideways like a crab. Linus raised his hand above his head and let Malloy see the flash of it as he touched the button to spring the

217

blade. Then, quickly, he lowered the knife so that it couldn't be seen by anyone any longer.

He stayed close to the woman's back, letting Malloy know with winks and smiles that if Malloy dared lay a hand on him, or even came too close, Linus would add her to his list of victims before Malloy could stop him. They shuffled down the tile corridor on the way to the Flushing trains.

When they reached the platform the woman went to sit down on the end of a bench that was nearly fully occupied. Linus left her side and nipped from one waiting rider to another, pretending to be a broken-field runner, pretending to be a dancer in some New York musical, grinning like a clown or a madman every time Malloy seemed about to make a try at him.

The local train was coming. Linus stopped dancing around and placed himself close to a little man with a wizened face like that of a petulant lap dog. He watched Malloy's every step.

"Hey, hey, hey," Linus crooned softly and pursed his lips in the form of an insulting kiss.

The wizened man didn't seem to hear, or pretended that the remark wasn't intended for him.

"We can still negotiate this, kid," Malloy said.

"Oh, yeah? What's your offer? Life?"

"That's right. You keep on running and someone—maybe not me—but someone—will bring you down. If that someone's a cop with a gun he might just take your life. Blow it right out the back of your head."

They were speaking as softly as two lovers. Actually they were reading each other's lips as much as really hearing the words. The little man didn't seem to be paying any attention. Malloy tensed up as the train screeched into the station just an arm's length away. The doors opened. Linus hooked the little man's arm and moved forward into the car with him, then turned him around so they were both facing Malloy who was about to step inside.

Malloy could see the knife held low, the blade pointed up toward the little man's kidneys. Linus grinned and held up his hand, palm out like a traffic cop as the doors closed in Malloy's face.

Malloy went to sit on an empty bench. He took the bulky transceiver from the pocket of his overcoat and triggered the transmission switch.

The man on the desk picked up almost immediately.

"This is O'Hara," he said.

"Malloy. I'm on the Grand Central platform of the 7 going east. The local just went through. I want you to put that train on the layover track at Vernon."

"Give me a reason, Malloy."

"I've got the Monopoly Killer on the run."

"You've got it," O'Hara's voice came back, flat and without emotion, thin as a blade cutting through the snap and crackle of atmospherics. "You want me to pull the plug on it altogether?"

"No, no. That'll just scare him into a hole. Just shunt it off and hold it until the express goes through, then put it back on the route. But, O'Hara, I want you to tell the driver on the express to make a stop at Hunter's Point."

"Will do," O'Hara said. His voice had grown weak. "Is there—"

"Say again," Malloy said into the mouthpiece. Nothing came back to him. He shook the transceiver and tried again, but he wasn't receiving any more and doubted if he were sending, either.

When the 7 Express rolled in Malloy got aboard.

Now he'd really done it, really got away from the Transit cop. Linus sat on the seat and looked impressive. Then he started to giggle. Then he started to roar. The pain behind his eyes had risen to a point where it was a kind of ecstasy. A man with Oriental eyes, red hair, and freckles across a flat-bridged nose stared at Linus, checking out just how crazy he was. Linus snapped his head around and glared at the man. He wanted to play the eye challenge game again. He wanted to root that sucker to the spot, and maybe he'd slip the knife in him. Leave him lying along the trail of his escape. Give Malloy something more to think about.

The freckle-faced man wanted out of the combat, but he couldn't seem to tear his eyes away. This kid couldn't let go. Fear rose up in his throat. Then, suddenly, Linus grew bored with it all. He crossed his eyes and stuck out his tongue, then started laughing again, feeling magnanimous.

The train slowed approaching Vernon. It wasn't supposed to. Ordinarily he wouldn't have noticed. Any number of things could demand that the train delay its trip by a minute or two. But he was hyper, ready to react to any least thing out of the ordinary or expected.

The train moved off into a lay-up track running parallel to the main line. The sides complained as they scraped the linkage of the undercarriages making the tight curve. It came to rest, the motors chugging softly.

After no more than a minute or two the train started up again and got back on track, but now the 7 Express was running before it.

At Hunter's Point the Express made the unscheduled stop and Malloy got out. He placed himself behind a steel pier at the very end of the platform. When the Local entered the station Malloy caught a glimpse of Linus with his face pressed up close to the graffiti-smeared window. Malloy waited till the last minute to see if Linus would leave the train, then stepped aboard the last car.

Linus was satisfied that Malloy wasn't on his heels. He could relax until the train reached 74th and Roosevelt out

220

in Jackson Heights before changing to either the Sixth or Eighth Avenue train for the trip back to Lexington and Third, where he could go into the tunnels and make his way back to Grand Central and find his hidey-hole there.

He picked up an abandoned newspaper lying on the seat beside him and began reading the front page. No news of him. No howls out of Seagrave. Well, he'd just have to do something to grab their attention again. He patted the butt of the gun where it lay cradled against his stomach.

Malloy walked the length of the train, opening each door, stepping out on the rocking platforms, closing it behind him, then opening the next. Each time he stood outside the shells of the cars the wind of passage buffeted him. It made him feel good. He closed his eyes and imagined himself on the deck of a ship. He knew it was really nothing similar, but it was the closest he could get.

He rocked easily on his feet, holding on to the handle of the door that led into the car occupied by Linus. Malloy could see the kid reading the paper. Then Linus looked up sharply as though he'd sensed Malloy so close. Malloy jerked back in plenty of time, seeing the sharp tightening of the neck muscles, knowing what Linus was going to do.

A funny quirk of reflection caught Malloy's eye. From a certain angle, looking through the window of the car door, he could see Linus reflected in the glass cover on an advertisement. There was a reflective spot amid all the sprayed graffiti that framed a miniature of Linus.

He did not return to his reading. He seemed all tight and ready to fight or run. He rolled up the newspaper and stuffed it into his back pocket, then settled back against the seat again.

Malloy decided to take him when they pulled into 74th and Roosevelt. He waited with his back against the car, holding on to the handle with one hand, the chain guards

221

with the other. Now that he'd made up his mind to capture Linus out here, where the station wouldn't be crowded, where he might be able to get to a cop with greater ease, where he might at least capture the attention of other people less apt to turn away, he felt the nightmare fear starting up in a circle around his heart.

He waited through 52nd and 61st, through 69th and along the stretch to 74th. The train pulled in. Malloy took a quick look. Linus was looking at his hands in an idle way, relaxed and languid. There was no one else on the car. It would be easy. The doors started to slide open the minute the train came to a full stop. Malloy slammed open the end door and was running toward the place where Linus had been sitting just a moment before.

For something had alerted him. Perhaps the reflection had worked its magic both ways and Linus had seen the edge of a hiding man out on the train coupling sills, and if any man was waiting out there, who else could it have been but Malloy? Perhaps as Malloy had held onto the handle Linus had noticed some movement of it. Whatever had sparked the new flight, he'd been out the door before it was all the way back, running along the pedestrian tunnels.

He jumped aboard the E going back into Manhattan. Malloy was seconds behind him, but so out of breath and weary that he couldn't even make the necessary moves to back Linus into a corner.

There were empty seats on both sides of the aisle. One was next to a working man with heavy hands that dangled, work-worn and powerful, between his knees. The other was next to a young woman dressed in running pants and a hooded sweat shirt. Her hair was pulled back and caught with a rubber band, so that she looked girlish and vulnerable. Linus chose to sit next to her and, as Malloy moved toward him, he pulled the knife and bared the blade.

The cars slammed against the rails, taking Malloy off balance just a second before he committed himself to attack.

222

Linus had the point at the girl's side before Malloy could recover.

She was smart enough to freeze, only her eyes moving to see why the young man sat next to her so awkwardly. She didn't really have to see the knife to know that she was threatened. The man across the aisle reflexively clenched his fists, his eyes widening as the shot of adrenaline roused him.

Malloy sat down next to him and put his hands in the pockets of his coat. He leaned forward, his eyes directly on Linus.

"It's just between you and me, isn't it, Linus?"

"Yeah?" Linus said doubtfully.

"I mean it's me you think tried to play a trick on you at the church. Right?"

Linus wouldn't answer him. His eyes blinked rapidly.

"That's why you wanted to stab Irma. The nurse. That's why you wanted to hurt somebody I cared about. To hurt me."

"Go fuck yourself with the fancy dialogue, Malloy. I know the game."

Malloy closed his eyes very slowly, then opened them, a gesture of saintlike patience, proof of his willingness to repeat his arguments as often as necessary to make Linus understand that he was not out to do him an injury.

"There's no reason to bring anyone else into this, Linus," Malloy said.

"Don't do that!" Linus said sharply.

"Do what?"

"Keep calling me by name."

"That's your name, isn't it? Isn't Linus your name?"

"Don't do it. I know about that trick."

"Trick?"

"Cops are taught those tricks. Get the loony's confidence. Get the crazy thinking they're friends. Isn't that the way it goes?"

"Ahh, Jesus, you're running me in circles," Malloy said helplessly.

There was a moment of silence as they both contemplated the remark in light of the chase they were engaged upon, and both started laughing at the same moment, Malloy not really laughing, not for real, pretending to, and hoping for Linus's laughter to distract him just long enough for Malloy to reach across and . . .

Linus stopped laughing and made a motion with the arm and hand that held the knife. He didn't push it any harder against the side of the girl, but his intent was clearly proclaimed.

"Hey, stop scaring the lady," Malloy said.

"Don't con me, Malloy."

"Throw the knife away, tough guy," Malloy snapped.

"You're a joke," Linus replied in a slow, insulting drawl.

"Toss it away. Don't use a girl as a shield."

"Go fuck yourself."

"I'll give you a head start out the door."

The young woman's eyes were flickering everywhere now. Malloy was afraid that might be an indication she was about to panic or faint.

The train was pulling into Queens Plaza.

"Let her move over, Linus," Malloy said.

"You're a comedian," Linus answered. "Lady?"

"Yes?" she said in a surprisingly strong voice.

"Lady, you're going to stand up when I stand up. You're going to stay close to me. You hear?"

"Yes."

"You understand what I'll do if you try to run?"

"Yes."

"Okay," Linus nodded.

The woman started to stand up as she said, "Now?"

The train was still moving. Linus snatched at her sleeve and yelled, "Not yet!"

The girl jerked her arm away. "You said to stand up,"

224

she shrieked louder than she had to. The workingman made a clumsy lunge across the aisle as the young woman gave Linus her elbow right in the throat. The doors opened and people came into the car. The knife clattered to the floor. Malloy reached out a foot and kicked it away, then started to reach for it as two new passengers hurried to capture one vacant seat. One of them, a big woman, slammed her knee into the side of Malloy's head. Her eyes were narrowed; she was not about to lose the seat she had them fixed on. The young woman in the running pants, no longer threatened by the knife, was reaching for Linus, meaning to hurt him if she could.

Linus fell backwards, then eeled his way through the tangle. He was out the door and running again. Malloy was slow to take up the chase. He was ready to let Linus go away and hide himself. In time he'd be found. But in the meanwhile what would the kid do? How many would he kill? He might even go after Irma again.

Of course Malloy never had a chance of letting go. He chased Linus down the platform at Queens Plaza, dodging the stairways, and finally pulled up short. Linus was there, ahead of him, leaning against a post, head down, mouth open, one hand clutched to his side. His wound was hurting him as badly as the old bullet scars were hurting Malloy. He looked up, head still dangling, and grinned. Malloy started walking toward him. Then Linus showed him the gun.

It was true, Malloy thought; a sudden shock makes you feel as though your guts have turned to water. It had never been this bad before. Not even when the gunman had brought him down in that black alley. Linus turned away, and almost casually jumped down onto the roadbed. He started walking along the tracks into the yawning tunnel.

Malloy went down to the very end. He took his time sitting down on the filthy edge of the platform, and then sliding off onto the gravel between the tracks. He turned and faced the tunnel mouth. God, it was black. For a brief moment Linus passed within the weak illumination of a work lamp. He turned at that moment. The light was a thin gruel on his face and hair. He smiled. Then he was gone.

Malloy started walking into the dark, the muscles of his belly wincing from unfelt, invisible blows.

44.

It was black as pitch in the tunnels, except for the glow of small colored signal lights and the blue lamps that marked the work phones. They gleamed dully in the dark like the eyes of beasts. Far away along the tracks there was a high singing, the song of the train on the rails.

Linus was familiar with the tunnels. He knew where the safety islands used by the repairmen pierced the tunnel walls. Many times he'd stood in them like a god on some Egyptian temple wall, arms crossed across his chest as the train sped through. Sometimes startled passengers had seen him there, standing so eerily composed.

Malloy knew the tunnels too. They were a necessary part of his job. Many times he'd been called upon to walk the dark line searching for someone lost or fallen, killed and tossed aside by accident or design. They were a part of his

227

personal therapy as well. He faced up to the yawning black mouths the way soldiers faced up to repeated landings on hostile beaches, the way adventurers climbed the mountain once again after a narrow escape from death.

Always before, however, the dangers lurking in the inky passages had been those of his imagination, terrifying enough, but ultimately unreal. Now a madman with a gun was running scared and vicious just in front of him.

Malloy slowed down, his heart beating fiercely in his chest, echoing in his throat. His mouth was dry. Little pinpoints of light gathered in the corners of his eyes and swam around in the dark. They were as brilliant as tinsel or chromium confetti. His legs were tired. The time seated on the train, trying to convince Linus, had given him no real rest. He was no longer young enough to expect his body to bounce back from hard exertion. He had a burst or two left, but recovery was longer coming and shallower when it came.

Linus had hearing like a fox. Malloy's feet no longer pounded in shuffling, running rhythm behind him. He slowed to a walk. His own lungs seared with each breath he took. The wound, though healed, had taken something from him. That and the fact that he no longer ate so regularly or so well now that Peg was dead.

Up ahead the singing turned to a rattling rumble, the snare drum of wheels and rails. A tiny light could be seen. This was a long, straight stretch of tunnel. A train was approaching.

The N train roared through the tunnel on the way from Queens to Manhattan. Its headlamp grew larger and larger. It rushed past the maintenance well in the wall where Linus had plastered himself against the tug of the rushing air.

As the train swept past Malloy, he had the sudden desire to give himself up to the suction that pulled at him with gentle persuasion. It was the sort of attraction experienced by some people standing on high towers or the edges of great precipices. When the N was gone, hurrying under the East River, Malloy got off the ledge very slowly, feeling his way with his foot, the other planted firmly on the concrete, one hand grasping the guard rail with all his strength.

Like an old man, he thought. That gave him some sort of angry energy. He went along the tunnel at a faster pace, heels clipping the ties in a steady, military rhythm. Suddenly he stopped. There was no sound up ahead. Was Linus in ambush?

Malloy proceeded with great caution. He took out his flashlight. There might be one chance in a hundred that he could dazzle Linus with it before the kid could set his sights. It was a hope.

There wasn't a snick of sound up ahead. Then he heard the hushing, slithery slide of something. A footstep? Cloth rubbing against cloth as the man with the gun set himself? He punched the switch on the flashlight. The beam snapped out like a sword blade. There was nothing in its light except the wall. Over there a connection box. Over there a guard rail.

He could feel the bullets slamming into him. Why the hell didn't Linus shoot? Malloy had gambled with the light and lost. Over there a pool of water no bigger than the palm of a man's hand, and a rat drinking from it. Running off a moment after the beam of light turned its glaring eyes to rubies. Over there a glistening sheen of water on the wall. Over there a set of metal steps leading up.

Malloy knew that it led up to the eastern pier of the Queensboro Bridge.

The tunnel-dweller was seeking the air. Why? Was it simply so that he would have light enough from the street and the bridge to shoot Malloy when he emerged?

It seemed to take a long time for him to climb the iron ladder. He came out into the night air, the wind whistling up along the river, tearing at his coat. A cold wind, the last late breath of winter. Halfway across the bridge he could see a figure stumbling along. He knew it couldn't be anyone but Linus. He started after him, picking his feet up and laying them down hard, continuing the steps along the bridge. Cars went by, creating little eddies of air.

Linus examined his condition as he ran. His human condition. He'd been a loner, true enough. A loner among loners. But there had been a few friends, people who recognized him and raised their hands in greeting as he passed. People for whom he felt nothing but amused contempt. He regarded a few with a kind of affection, thready and pale. He was afraid to invest much more than that. There had been Peg. He'd liked her, really liked her. She shouldn't have driven him to violence. It had been wrong of her. He'd had a few laughs with Bo Wango and Reverend Moss and Maud's Sister, and there'd even been times when he'd felt kindly toward Eddie B, wet brain and all.

There was no place in the tunnels for him any more. They would never find the courage to do much more than blow horns at him and keep him from sleeping, and would, in time, even give up such petty irritations as those. Still, they'd never speak with him again, never smile or raise a hand in greeting. They'd walk past him as though he weren't even there. There was nothing more alone than being an outcast among the tunnel-dwellers.

Linus laughed bitterly and wiped his mouth with the back of his hand. The air was thick, scented with industrial smoke and automobile fumes. Up or down it was all the same. Over or under it was all rotten.

He turned right and stepped onto the footbridge leading to the tramway on Roosevelt Island. It was the last one of the night. Malloy didn't make it. He watched Linus being carried away, then wearily made his way afoot to the end of the bridge, running a little every now and then.

When the tram reached Second Avenue, Linus hopped

off and headed in the direction of the stations where he might get the trains running on the Lexington line or the BMT.

Malloy reached the end of the bridge. Linus was out of sight, but Malloy knew he was heading for the subways again. He flagged down a cruising cab and told him to drive to Lexington and 59th. He got lucky and spotted Linus going down into the BMT station. He paid the cabbie and went after Linus, making sure to keep a distance between them.

Linus took the first train going downtown. Malloy found a place in another car, where he hoped he wouldn't be seen. He didn't have any clear idea about what he could do now. The worst thing he could do would be to try and collar Linus again, or talk him into surrender where innocent people were about. Linus just might start spraying bullets all around.

He felt impotent, caught by a curious lack of energy far beyond the depletion of strength caused by the sporadic pursuit. With a sharp sense of recognition Malloy realized that, in the oddest way, he sympathized, or empathized with Linus. He saw in the boy one of the walking wounded, just as he knew himself to be in his secret heart.

Still, Linus must be taken.

The stations passed one by one. Fifth Avenue, 57th, Seventh Avenue.

"Ridin' on the Broadway Local," Linus sang softly, making up a song, pretending that he was one of those rich performers who stood on a stage with laser lights blasting around overhead, singing of their dissatisfaction with the society, and making two skillion bucks while doing so.

"Ridin' on the Broadway Local, goin' nowhere.

Ridin' on the subway, all alone.

Ridin' on the trains, seein' no one.

Ridin' on the Broadway Local, goin' home."

He let out a hard rock yell then, high-pitched, tuned to a

231

bat's ears, and laughed when a black man looked at him placidly, as though such things happened every day. The man smiled as though to say, "Oh, yeah, oh, yeah, I hear you."

Past 49th Street, Times Square, 34th, 28th—the local touched all the bases down the gut of Manhattan—23rd, Union Square, and 8th Street.

"Ridin', always ridin'," Linus sang softly to himself. "Runnin', always runnin'." The change of words seemed to startle him. He tossed his head from side to side, violently disagreeing with the destiny that had him riding lonely subways, and running, always running.

"No more, goddamn it, no more," he shouted.

"Right on, brother," the black man crooned.

Other people on the car, few and not so bold, looked at Linus sidelong.

Prince, Canal, then the long leg under the river again. This time on the way to Brooklyn.

Linus sang to himself, and sometimes he cursed. Most of the riders got off. Some shifted over to other cars, playing it safe. A few new riders, coming on the train, caught Linus's act and thought better of being part of his audience.

But the black man stayed on, shouting, "Right on!", and "Amen, brother!", whenever Linus yelled out his random defiance.

Linus got up and, fighting for his balance against the swaying of the car, still weak in the legs, he made his way down to the black man's end of the car. He stood in front of the smiling man with his legs spread wide apart and grinned down at him.

The train pulled into De Kalb.

The black man extended a hand palm up.

"I'm with you," he said.

Linus looked at the pink palm as though it were something alien. He lifted up his sweater and showed the black man his gun. The man's eyes grew wary and the smile left

232

his face; he clutched his hand into a fist, but it was a passive, pleading motion, not an aggressive one.

"Easy, brother," he breathed.

"I'm not your brother," Linus replied.

"Whatever you say."

Jesus Christ, Malloy thought, as he watched what was going on in the next car. Somebody touched him off. Somebody got Linus stirred again.

Malloy could see the butt of the gun hard up against the kid's belly, his hand hovering near it as though waiting for the draw to be called.

Christ, I'm not ready for it yet, Malloy thought, and got up and went to the end door, keeping himself hidden behind the frame as he prepared himself.

"I say you're a nigger bastard and a yellow-bellied son of a bitch," Linus said in a flat voice.

The black man shrugged shoulders powerful even now, at his age.

"Ahhh, why do you want to abuse my pride this way, man?" he asked sadly. "I've got no gun."

The train pulled into Pacific.

Linus raised his hands above his head.

"It's right there. Why don't you try and take it?"

The black man's hands twitched, but stayed in his lap.

The doors closed and the train went on.

"Is that thing really loaded?" the man asked.

"Why don't you try and find out?"

"What kind of game you playing?"

"No game. This is for real."

"There was a time I could have taken that gun away from you, no sweat. You know that?"

"So what's stopping you?"

233

"Was a time when I had nobody to care about, but myself."

"You begging off?"

"Now I've got a wife and children."

Linus lowered his arms. They were getting tired. He put one hand in his pocket and placed his palm on the butt of the gun with the other.

"Lost your chance," he said.

Malloy took a peek. Things were worse. He could see that. Linus had his hand on the gun. Malloy would have to move. He opened up the door of his car and stepped out onto the metal sills leading to the next one. He closed the door behind him as the train pulled into Union Street. A couple of people got on. When the train pulled out Malloy opened the door to the car in which Linus and the black man were confronting each other. Linus never glanced Malloy's way.

"Is that the trouble, son?" the black man said softly. "Ain't you got nobody?"

Linus pulled the gun out of his belt. Malloy took three steps and wrapped his arms around Linus from behind. The black man clamped his huge hand around Linus's wrist and squeezed. Linus yelled, because of the pain of the grip, or in angry frustration. He thrashed one way and another as the gun clattered to the floor.

"Let him go, man," the black man ordered Malloy. "Stay out of this."

There was outrage in his voice. Malloy was intruding on a matter that the black man considered private. He had been playing his game, ready to strike when his pleas had lulled Linus into carelessness. If some stranger came to save his ass at the eleventh hour, how would he ever know if he'd had the courage to fight for his own life?

He dragged at Malloy's arm. It was enough to allow Linus

234

to get away. The train rushed into 9th Street. The doors opened and Linus rushed out.

"You should have stayed the hell out of it, mister," the black man yelled at Malloy. "I didn't need no help. I didn't need none of your goddamn honky help."

Malloy didn't even bother to reply or to explain. He was out after Linus.

At least Linus was no longer armed. It pleased Malloy to know that he'd gone after him even though Linus held a gun in his fist.

Linus ran up the stairs to the outdoors, and Malloy followed.

45.

Smith and 9th Streets in South Brooklyn at eighty-seven and one half feet above street level is the highest point in the entire subway system. Linus ran along the streets to it with Malloy behind him, then he leaned on the rail surrounding the platform looking out toward the towers of Manhattan. The black cardboard shapes stood out against the city-shine in the bowl of the sky. A thousand pinpoints of light pierced the stage setting. Linus turned and looked out into the harbor. Little automobiles, probing the dark on the expressway ahead with antennae of light, crept along. Below lay the Gowanus Canal and his old neighborhood, Red Hook.

Somewhere out in the night, somebody was making music or a music machine was playing. It was an old song. Linus knew it to be "Stardust," although it was a tune much before his time. He felt a wrenching longing for something he'd never known. He heard Malloy's footsteps behind him. They stopped.

"You're not going to grab my arm, are you?" Linus asked.

"What?" Malloy said.

"You're not going to hang a 'come along' on me like I was some goddamn shoplifter, are you?"

Malloy didn't speak. He was waiting for his breath to come back.

Finally he said, "Are you going to go running off again?"

"You asking for promises?"

"Well?"

"We going to talk about promises?"

"I didn't know that cop was on my tail."

Linus made a noise of disbelief, blowing air through his nose.

"Have it your way. Whatever. There was no reason for you to go after Irma."

"She's yours, isn't she?"

"No, she's not mine. We don't own each other."

"You sleep with her, don't you?"

"Sure," Malloy said softly, sensing that Linus meant nothing smutty with his curiosity. There was an odd longing in his voice when the kid went on.

"In her nice sweet-smelling bed?"

"Sure."

"I sleep alone in a dirty corner of a steam tunnel."

"I've got no tears for you. It doesn't have to be that way."

"Get a job?"

"Something like that."

"That's not it."

"Maybe not."

"Not all of it."

"I know."

"If I tell you, will you listen?"

"Yeah."

237

"It's not just getting a job. It's not just finding someone to care whether you live or die. It's not just feeling lost inside your head. It's everything. It's every goddamn thing."

"We better be moving along. I'm tired. You must be tired. We got a way to go."

"We going to Police Plaza?"

"Why not?"

Malloy touched his elbow. Linus started.

"You know what, Malloy?"

"What?"

"I went to the library once. I went through the newspapers looking for my birth notice. There wasn't any."

"Come on," Malloy said, and put his hand on Linus again. The boy jerked away. He moved to the right as though he were going to run again, setting his hands on the railing as he spun around to face Malloy, his feet scrabbling up the posts as though he meant to kick out. Malloy moved in close. There was a moment when neither one seemed to believe what was happening. Then Malloy made a grab as Linus went over. It had happened just like that. So goddamn easy.

Just like that Linus went over the rail and got all busted to hell and dead on the pavement eighty-seven and one half feet below.

Malloy became aware of the painful grip of his hands on the rail. He stared down at the body. It looked like a dead cat.

"For God's sake, you didn't have to do that," Malloy whispered.

46.

Spring was in New York and no more looking back at winter. The sun poured down on the city. It poured down on the uplifted face of Irma Sweet, having her day off from the slaughter house, sitting on the steps of the Metropolitan Museum of Art, head back, eyes closed.

Malloy kissed her on the cheek and sat down beside her. She opened one eye to make certain it was him.

"I'll call a cop," she said.

"I'm a cop," he said. "Sort of."

She opened both eyes and looked full into his face.

"You know what, Malloy?"

"What?"

"You really have got to find a barber with a shop on the street."

He grinned.

"It's spring," she said.

"I noticed."

"You going to stay above ground for a while?"

She kissed him on the mouth before he could say no.

Eddie B and Willie the Walker sat on the bench in the station at the 57th Street station, BMT.

Eddie B looked doubtful. He hugged himself with his thin arms and looked at the staircase leading to the outdoors with suspicion.

"Well, I don't know," he said. "I just don't know."

"Come on," Willie pleaded, "it's warm and green in the park."

"I don't much like going out on the streets."

"There's nothing to be afraid of."

Eddie B still hesitated.

"Nothing up there will hurt you. I wouldn't steer you wrong. Honest. We could go to the zoo."

"Yeah?" Eddie B's face lit up.

"Sure. Okay?"

Eddie B hesitated only a moment longer; then he grinned and stood up. Willie the Walker stood up too, and linked his arm through Eddie B's.

They walked up the stairs. The sunlight lit up their hair as they went up and out into the morning.

R. Wright Campbell is also the author of *The Spy Who Sat and Waited*—an American Book Awards nominee—*Circus Couronne, Where Pigeons Go to Die* and *Killer of Kings*. He is also well-known as a screen writer, his 1957 film, *Man of a Thousand Faces*, earning him an Oscar nomination. He lives in Carmel, California.